I0822634

The Crystal Palace Murder

By Johanna M. Rieke

First English edition published in 2022

First published in 2020 by Frankfurter Literaturverlag, Frankfurt, Germany. Translated from the original German by Bryan Stone.

Paperback ISBN 978-1-78705-993-1
Hardcover Special Edition – 978-1-80424-096-0
ePub ISBN 978-1-78705-994-8
PDF ISBN 978-1-78705-995-5

MX Publishing, 335 Princess Park Manor, Royal Drive, London, N11 3GX
www.mxpublishing.com

Cover design by Brian Belanger
Translation by Bryan Stone

Dedicated to Bryan, my dear husband, who published a seminar paper in Switzerland in 2017 which delivered the inspiration for this work

A Foreword by Dr. John Watson

The reader will well remember my description, in 'The Final Problem¨, of how Holmes and I travelled to Meiringen, in Switzerland, how we there encountered Professor Moriarty, and how, as we then believed, Holmes and Moriarty fell to their deaths in the Reichenbach Falls. My grief at the violent death of my closest friend can be readily imagined, mitigated as it may have been, by the knowledge that Holmes had kept his word; he would rid the world, even at the cost of his own life, of a dangerous and malevolent criminal. After the inevitable enquiries, I was able to return., to London, sadly alone, but to be greeted by my loving wife Mary. It would be some time before I could take up my notes again, and set out, as I tried to do in 'The Final Problem'. Even then, my head was ringing with questions which Holmes would, as I thought, now never answer. Indeed, why were we in Meiringen? My uneasiness reflected that I had felt, even there, that I had surely not heard the whole story.

Again immersed in my practice, and with Mary beside me, I tried to find solace. The tragedy of my wife's death was therefore doubly devastating. You will, dear reader, understand my emotional reaction when, after three years, I found Holmes standing before me. He could tell me little, except that he had escaped death and had left the Falls to flee, ten miles over the mountain, and to disappear. His account of this absence was then included in my story of 'the Empty House'. As you will see, I was soon to learn more, and this in a situation where Professor Moriarty's death would reveal just how deeply the jealousies of the European nations were poisoning our world. Holmes knew, and was aware that the vacuum of Moriarty's death would be filled.

On an earlier visit to Basle, Switzerland, to investigate the death of a young Englishman, we saw already in Moriarty's networks tensions and rivalries. That case will, I hope, if it is published, help to show why Holmes was already suspicious and alert. We first heard there of the elusive 'German Knife-Grinder', his name coming from his favourite disguise, who had Moriarty's confidence but whose ultimately loyalties were far from clear. Where was he now?

For three years I heard no more of all these things than were in the daily papers, as they reported the tensions of an uneasy world, but it was clear that Holmes, if unable to speak, had not been idle. These and many more thoughts occupied my mind, as I walked out on a summer afternoon in Kensington.

Dr. Watson remembers

You will, dear reader, surely recall the unusual and dramatic summer of 1894. The weather in London was quite remarkable, with exceptionally high temperatures through the day, and then, almost every evening, a torrential downpour. It was scarcely surprising, therefore, that the air became insufferably unpleasant, humid and heavy, and this quickly came to dominate the whole atmosphere of daily life. Those who could, avoided every exertion and sought relief in the many parks and gardens.

On this afternoon of July 28th, I too was thankful, in the early afternoon, to find myself in a cool alley of trees, walking slowly in their shade, seemingly in a green tunnel as their crowns met over my head. This offered protection from the relentless sun above me, as I walked slowly and reflectively along the central walk of the West London and Westminster Cemetery. For readers who do not know this place of peaceful rest in our busy capital, I should explain that more than fifty years ago, as the rapid growth of the population became apparent, this cemetery was generously planned and laid out. The original ambitious plan for a unique wooded park was never fulfilled, but that which was created is today recognised thankfully by the residents of Kensington and Westminster, as a worthy place of rest for their loved ones.

As I came nearer to my objective, I saw the octagonal chapel, with its domed roof flanked by a classical colonnade, looming larger in my field of view. Inevitably my thoughts went back to the way in which my dear Mary had often expressed, in a romantic enthusiasm, her appreciation of this scene, where the chapel inevitably reminded one of a diminutive version of the square of St Peter's in Rome. She had come to love this setting during many visits to the cemetery, as in the time before our marriage she had been employed as a companion to Mrs. Forrester, whose late husband had some years before been laid to rest near this spot in the West London and Westminster Cemetery.

But now I had to leave the central walk, turning into a narrower path on the left. A few paces further, I turned again to the right, and so I had again the colonnaded chapel before me. Here, the path I took, which led over freshly cut lawns, was narrow, and now I was again out of the shade and in the full force of the sun. However, my step did not falter. The chapel with its honey-coloured stone seemed to catch and radiate the warmth of the sunshine. It came to my mind that only a few observers might be aware that beneath the chapel there was a group of catacombs, quiet dark underground tombs, in which many a past Londoner had now found a last resting place.

Occupied with this thought, I had passed the grave of the distinguished architect and journalist, George Godwin. When we think that that gentleman had been largely responsible for laying out South Kensington and Earls Court as we know them today, and was an influential member of the Royal Commission on the living conditions of the poor, and that he also wrote several works performed in the theatres of his day, we may conclude that he was a remarkably able person with a wide variety of interests. Some may know him as the editor of the influential journal "The Builder," in which architects, engineers and also lovers of art found an interest. His monument has two grieving figures, representing faith and mercy, and a portrait medallion. Above these is a sculptured oil-lamp, which stands for eternal life.

With these reflections I had now arrived where I wished to be. Compared to memorials such as I have described, this one was modest: a light-coloured stone of moderate size, rounded at the top, where a branch in blossom but broken, was engraved, and had another budding branch growing from it, but from which also another young branch is springing out, though already broken. Beneath the engraving are the names of my dear wife, Mary, and of our son, Hamish. I knelt down, and, as always, laid a small bunch of flowers before the stone. We had so greatly looked forward to our child as the symbol of our affection. The perspective of becoming a father had even calmed my deep sadness following what I had believed to be Holmes' tragic death at the Reichenbach Falls. I had repeatedly thought of the flight through Switzerland to Meiringen, at the end of which the inevitable final confrontation must come, between my friend Sherlock Holmes and the master criminal, Professor Moriarty. I had found no respite for my tormented mind as I journeyed, sadly and alone, back to London in May 1891. Mary alone had understood the emptiness I had felt.

I even tried to hide this dark memory from my loyal readers of the Strand Magazine. It was regrettable, indeed quite reprehensible, that Professor Moriarty's brother had attempted then to portray his brother's life and work in a better light.

This was indeed done at the cost of the good name of my friend, Sherlock Holmes. I had to act; I felt obliged to break my silence and to describe to our public what had really happened. You may, dear readers, well remember how I published the account which you found under the title of "The Final Problem," which appeared last year in the Strand Magazine, and which set an end to the perfidious slights being put about by Moriarty's brother. That I could in this way protect and defend the good name of my friend was profoundly uplifting to me. My whole attitude was the better for it. I began again to look forward to the future.

There came then, however, the blow, as Mary's delivery made itself prematurely apparent, long before it was due. The doctor in me, who had seen many things, was at once in alarm. Although I had taken her at once to St. Bartholomew's hospital, there was nothing that could be done to avert the disaster. Our little Hamish would never see the light of day. And within a few days, my dear Mary had followed him there where there is no return, and I was now to be alone. It was devastating, and I was angry and bitter at my own helplessness. I felt again a dreadful emptiness rising in me, and, despite real and widespread sympathy from all sides, I knew that there was now no consolation, no comfort.

I plunged into my work, fighting in this way against the pain and hopelessness that filled me, attended to my practice and my visits, and I offered my help at St Bartholomew's, or otherwise read professional medical papers and works. Up to a point this intensive activity really helped. During twelve months I had regularly visited the Brompton Cemetery, and I felt that it was gradually getting easier. But easy it was not; it was a painful experience every single time. The pain of bereavement eased, but the loneliness did not.

You may, dear reader, try to imagine, what mixture of emotions overwhelmed me, when in my practice in Kensington, in early April, there appeared, quite unannounced, Sherlock Holmes himself, that dear person whom I had believed, since Meiringen, to be dead, and I admit that it was at first too much for my constitution. He had returned, just in time to solve the mystery surrounding the death in London of the Honourable Ronald Adair. In doing so he had again ensured that a murderer, and a leading member of Moriarty's old network, would now receive his due punishment. You, dear reader, know of this circumstance, and the case, from the story I published under the name of "The Empty House." As I had spent that April evening with Holmes, I began to feel again something of the old magic which had existed between us, as we pursued our adventures together.

Time had now again elapsed, and only a few days before my visit to the cemetery, Holmes had called, presenting again his sympathies, and gently asking me whether I would like to share with him the rooms we had so long known together at 221B, Baker Street. It was a tempting invitation, but I had hesitated to give him an answer. I had hoped that I might again be the trusty, loyal, energetic friend I had been before. Indeed, I hoped that my meditation at Mary's grave might have helped me, but I still felt very unsure of myself. Indeed, I was less convinced of my own state of mind than I had been before.

Standing at the grave, occupied with my own thoughts, I heard the crunching sound of wagon wheels on the gravel path. Turning to look at the chapel, I saw the reason. Another sad procession was on its way to the chapel, with an imposing black hearse drawn by four black horses moving slowly forwards. The black-feathered headpiece on each horse waved slowly back and forth with their movement. The black hanging drapes scarcely swung. I found this spectacle intrusive, breaking into my thoughts, and so I turned back, to face Mary's grave and to whisper, "I will soon be back."

I turned again and walked briskly through the churchyard to the central arcade, and was now pleased to reach the triumphal arch, which marked the entrance on Richmond Road.

221B Baker Street once more

I had not long to wait before I could hail, with my walking stick, a free hansom. It was my intention to return to my practice and spend the remainder of the afternoon reading a newly arrived medical journal. As I climbed into the cab, however, something changed my mind. Without thinking, I said to the driver, without hesitation, '221B Baker Street'

The spontaneous decision had ensured that I sacrifice an undoubtedly valuable and instructive afternoon, which would have been however without charm and probably boring. I was pleased with myself. I leaned back to enjoy the journey.

I now stood at the door, which I had known so well. I grasped the polished brass knocker and announced my presence. It was not long before Mrs. Hudson opened the heavy door to find me there, and I saw her always-motherly face light up. I wanted to greet her, to ask how Holmes was, and whether he was at home. I could not, for she offered an immediate sigh of relief and said at once, "Oh, Dr. Watson, you are a gift from Heaven, please come in".

She followed these few words with a gesture, and I accepted her invitation. As I stood in the hall, I heard the melancholy and deeply unmusical sound of a violin being played with all the pain and discord that only Holmes could achieve. My question, whether Holmes was in, was answered. The question must be, why he could so painfully maltreat this extraordinary instrument, which he had always claimed was a Stradivarius, bought at a pawnshop on the Tottenham Court Road, for 55 shillings. I knew that he could play it as a virtuoso, when he was of such a mind.

When he did not, it was for one of two completely different reasons. He was either fully occupied with a problem, and his violin was a means whereby he supported his reasoning, or he was without a case or some other intellectual challenge, and his active mind could not stand the boredom. But now Mrs. Hudson had come to join me. We looked at one another, and both then looked anxiously up at the door at the top of the stairs. Suddenly all went completely quiet. Our expressions relaxed somewhat, and we looked again in some suspicion. But it was not long, before Holmes again started his frightful cacophony, and I heard Mrs. Hudson's sigh of anguish beside me. I asked her, in all sympathy, "Has this been going on long, Mrs. Hudson?"

She nodded to me and answered, almost sobbing, "I cannot describe to you, how happy I was, to know that Mr. Holmes had not met his death in Switzerland, and again when he came back to London to take up his old life. But I must admit that this fearful noise on the violin, at all times of day and night, is making terrible demands on my nerves. Yes, even in the night I am no longer safe from his scratching away. He has only stopped when I brought him his meals. Today, however, he has touched neither his breakfast nor his lunch. There was not even then a pause in his dreadful playing. Oh, Dr. Watson, it makes me deeply sorry, that I say such things about Mr. Holmes, but…."

She could say no more, for she broke into heavy sobbing, so that the tears rolled down her cheeks. I drew my fresh pocket-handkerchief, and offered it to her, a gesture which she gratefully accepted. I offered a few words of comfort, and I saw that she was recovering her composure.

I then said to her, "Dear Mrs. Hudson, I will go straight up and see whether my presence can deter him from his playing." My words had the necessary effect. I saw a weak, but grateful, smile come to her features. I looked at her reassuringly, and climbed the narrow stair.

At the living-room door, I waited and then knocked. I heard no answering invitation from Holmes, but neither did the violin sound stop. I resolved to enter. The feeling as I opened the door, was almost overpowering. There where I had so long shared in the rooms with Holmes, it was as if time had stood still during his long absence. The air was again filled with the scent of his tobacco, and with a smell of chemicals. Even with the curtains drawn, allowing only a diffuse light to enter, I saw the familiar objects, which were here so distinctive. There was his Persian slipper, in which he kept his tobacco; there was the coal-scuttle in which were his cigars. On the chimney piece I noticed his correspondence, secured as always by his pocket-knife, while on the small table there were the burns which his chemical experiments had caused, and the table still had its collection of flasks, retort glasses, pipettes, and various dark-brown bottles of chemicals.

All over the floor were piles of books, scattered papers, notes and old newspapers. And there, in the midst of this disorder, sat my friend, cross-legged on the sofa, his eyes closed, aggressively drawing his bow across his treasured violin. He had not dressed that morning, and was still in a long nightshirt, with, over that, a mouse-grey dressing gown hanging half open. His hair was unkempt, standing up wildly, and his normally striking chin showed an unshaven stubble. He had obviously not been aware of my presence, and so I spoke gently to him.

"I had come to pay you a visit, my dear friend. But, if I disturb, I will leave you in peace."

I came no further, for at the sound of my voice Holmes opened his eyes, let the violin and bow slide to one side, and jumped up from the divan, as if propelled by a spring. Two steps and he was with me, standing there and shaking my hand vigorously, while his left hand held my shoulder. His eyes burned, and he broke into a friendly smile as he said,

"Watson, my old friend, what an agreeable surprise! Please sit down and join me."

I moved a few books off the seat of the armchair, that on which I had so often sat before the chimney in the past, and sat down, while Holmes again made himself comfortable on the sofa, this time in his favourite tailor's posture. There was a short moment of silence. I felt his gaze wandering over me, taking in all details. Then, he spoke.

"It was very wise of you to seek company on this day, instead of sitting alone at home. What would you say if we were to go this evening to St James' Hall and listen to Schumann's Fourth Symphony? We could then afterwards take dinner at Simpson's, just as we did in the old days."

"Dear Holmes, that would be a wonderful idea," I answered enthusiastically.

I saw a satisfied smile on his face, as he then said to me, "With the weekend before us, and the fact that it may then be a long evening tonight, I would suggest that, if your practice will allow it, you might be my guest here in your old room in our dear old Baker Street digs, for the coming days."

This suggestion from Holmes was very tempting, and it might be easier, after a weekend together, for me to decide whether I could perhaps go back again to our former life together in Baker Street. My patients would be well looked after by my neighbour in Kensington, Dr. Smythe, if I asked his help. We had in the recent years often helped one another in this way. I therefore expected no difficulty, even at short notice. My decision was thus not difficult, and I told Holmes, not without real warmth, "That is a most gracious idea. I will accept your offer with the greatest of pleasure."

"Splendid, Watson. Then I suggest that you return quickly to Kensington and arrange all that is necessary. While you do that, I will wash, dress and eat something simple. I fear that my empty stomach might otherwise unpleasantly disturb the concert."

I was ready to leave, when I thought suddenly of the remark he had made on my arrival. “Holmes, I asked, what did you mean by saying it was wise not to spend this day alone?”

Holmes thought for a moment and then replied, “I think I am right in recalling that this is the anniversary of the death of your wife. I observe that you have today already visited the West London and Westminster Cemetery”.

I looked at my friend in surprise and asked. “How ever did you guess that?”

“Not guessed, Watson, deduced!” he replied, obviously rather irritated. There then followed an explanation.

“I first took advantage of the fact that you are most meticulous, especially in matters concerning your work. You always hold your consultations in the mornings, and then make your visits in the afternoon. You always have with you your doctor’s bag and your notebook, in which you note all that is relevant about your patients. When you start your round, this notebook is always in your left-hand jacket pocket. At the end of your visits, it is always in the right-hand pocket. Moreover, as you spoke to me on entering, I saw at once that you did not have your doctor’s bag with you. You might, of course, have left it in the entrance hall; but since your notebook is also not here, I conclude that you have made no visits to patients this afternoon.”

He continued.

"Even so, despite the very warm weather, you had been out this afternoon. It was surely not, in the first place, to visit me. Your trouser legs have unmistakeable signs of dust and also of grass cuttings. Then, under your shoe there is some dried earth, so you have been where there was moist grass and earth. The colour of the earth tells me that you were in the district of West Brompton. And with all due respect, I consider you too serious to have been amusing yourself in a park. Next, I consider your hands. As we shook hands, I observed that there was flower pollen upon them. There arose a slight smell of lilies, so you had been carrying flowers. Where are these flowers now? Or, more precisely, where might you have taken flowers? They would scarcely have been for a new friend, for I am well informed, that your grief at your wife's death still weighs very heavily upon you. My brother, Mycroft, had advised me of the tragic death of your wife during my absence from London. I did not have the precise date, but it was at the end of June last year. All these observations lead me to conclude that you were this afternoon at the West London and Westminster Cemetery to remember your late wife, and that you then decided to visit me."

I looked at him in quiet respect, before telling him, "Indeed it was so, Holmes, it was exactly as you describe."

We sat quietly together for a moment, before he suddenly said, "But now it is really time for you to go back to Kensington." I rose to leave, and while he retired to his bedroom, I went downstairs.

I heard him call me, and he said, “Watson, please tell Mrs. Hudson I will need warm shaving water, and perhaps she might bring me something quick from the kitchen. Oh, yes, and she will need to prepare your bed for tonight.” He was now quiet, and I smiled. He was now unlikely to play his violin tonight.

Both at St. James’ Hall, and at Simpson’s, I saw that Holmes, the “Great London Detective,” was not forgotten, despite his long absence from London. The concert was shown as sold out, yet in some way, we found ourselves with two excellent places in an available box. At Simpson’s, although we had no reservation and all seemed busy, my friend’s name seemed to open doors which would otherwise have remained closed.

During the dinner, we talked only about the concert we had attended. The original name of the work was “Symphonic Fantasy for a large orchestra,” and Holmes was in his element as he described its history and background. I learned from him that it was originally Schumann’s second symphony and was only named the fourth on account of its greatly delayed publication. Holmes then expounded upon the thematic connections between the individual movements, which are not separated by pauses. This detail was taken very seriously by some of Schumann’s critics, who claimed that he had no understanding of the severe rules then considered as applying to symphonic composition. Holmes also drew my attention to some passages, which recall parts of Beethoven’s Ninth Symphony, which are in the same key.

For my part, I was in no way able to match his careful and deliberate analysis of such a work; my contribution to the conversation was rather, that I had an ear for especially moving melodic passages, and their energetic, stimulating or indeed calming impulses, and that I have an ear more for those passages which conjure up for me particularly sensitive and gentle, even dreamlike emotions. But Holmes was satisfied that he could teach me more.

Later that evening, back at 221B, sitting together and provided with whisky and our tobacco, I asked whether Holmes was working on a new case. He told me that this was not so, and that this was leading him into a feeling of intense boredom. While he was lamenting that there was, since the death of Professor Moriarty, no challenge in London worthy of his detective abilities, I found an opportunity to ask him about the time when all, near and far, had accepted that he was indeed dead. At first, he said nothing, and simply played thoughtfully with the whisky glass in his hand. When, however, he did speak, it was apparent that he was choosing his words with great care.

"My dear Watson, it would be a great pleasure to tell you something of my time abroad. However, my oath and word of honour oblige me to complete silence on those matters. Perhaps one day it may be possible, but only when the time is ripe."

I nodded in agreement, but could scarcely conceal my disappointment, and muttered, "Then I will have naturally to exercise my patience."

There followed an uncomfortable silence in the room, which was finally broken as Holmes said, "If it would interest you, my old friend, I am free to tell you more about the continental journey which we undertook together."

I was, partly because of my disappointment, rather abrupt as I replied, "I scarcely think you can tell me more than I already know about that from my own observation. After all, I lived through it all at your side, and shared with you our flight from Professor Moriarty."

I saw how he was at first slightly irritated by my reply, but then he smiled and said, to my surprise, "Watson, concerning our journey to Switzerland, you are gravely in error. Admittedly, it is not your fault. I had suggested things to you throughout our journey which must inevitably lead you to this false conclusion."

I found this intensely disturbing. "Holmes, what is this false conclusion?"

"That the purpose of our journey on the continent was to flee from Professor Moriarty."

Back to the Past

What kind of statement was this? I was completely confused and could only look at Holmes without comprehension, before almost shouting at him,

"But Holmes! I do not understand! What can you mean when you claim that it was not a flight? I remember very well that evening when you came to me in Kensington on April 24, in 1891. You told me of attacks on your person, and how Professor Moriarty had come to you here in Baker Street, to tell you uncompromisingly that you should no longer disturb his enterprises. You then asked me if I could come at short notice with you to the continent.

"During our absence, the Metropolitan Police, with the aid of your collection of evidence, was to round up the criminal network of Professor Moriarty in London. That you should at this moment choose to be absent from the scene, and to leave London without any definite destination, left me with the natural suspicion that you saw the necessity, while this was going on, to be out of reach of Moriarty. As I agreed, after your explanation, to come with you, you gave me detailed instructions on how to reach Victoria station the following morning."

I paused to recall the events.

"When you left me, you chose the unconventional exit by way of our house's back garden and climbing over the garden wall. My journey to Victoria station involved, indeed, your brother

Mycroft, improbably dressed as a coachman and driving a hansom. You yourself came in the disguise of an old Italian priest, joining the train at the last minute. I consider that all of this behaviour can very properly be considered as a flight in concealment."

Somewhat out of breath, I looked at Holmes challengingly. He had nodded throughout as I spoke, and now he smiled in some amusement as he spoke again to me.

"My dear friend, please calm yourself. You have exactly thought and felt what I had suggested to you. You will therefore understand that your assumption that we must flee from Professor Moriarty, was the reaction I had intended. Despite this, it was not the truth. If my intention had been merely to hide from Professor Moriarty, I would have done that in London. But before you are again tempted to be angry with me, allow me to suggest that you refill your whisky glass, light a cigar, and listen as I tell you the whole truth of the affair."

Although still rather irritated, I took the advice of my friend and watched as he refilled his pipe. He leaned back in his chair, as though he could thus all the more comfortably recite his story, a remarkable story that I could never have imagined.

"In the winter of 1890, I was approached by the French Government, on a matter of the highest order. Without going into the details, it involved the theft of state papers. These papers contained statements which, in false hands, could have led directly to war with the Triple Alliance. That this was so made my investigation all the more delicate and difficult. However, by the spring of 1891, I had completed my task successfully, and could restore the papers without loss or damage to the French Government. This was a most satisfying outcome, but it revealed to me something, which in the end, would turn out to be of even greater importance. It supported a suspicion which I had had for some time, but which I could not confirm."

I looked at him tensely, waiting for him to continue, as he paused, and the pause gave his words even more weight.

"It became clear to me that the theft had occurred directly under the orders of Professor Moriarty. He was responsible for the theft, and so it became clear to me that the Professor, whom I had always seen as a Napoleon of crime, had not only a perfectly organised network in London, functioning with almost military precision, undoubtedly with its tentacles throughout Britain, but that he had a corresponding network in France. It took me only three weeks from learning of his involvement in the theft of the government papers to obtaining certainty that he had his French organisation. As you know, Watson, I had always known that Moriarty, who had an honourable public reputation as a master mathematician, could in practice never, even by me, be brought to book in connection with any given crime.

"He always operated even in London through intermediaries, under his then adjutant Colonel Sebastian Moran. Although this provided connections to a wide range of forgers, thieves, murderers and many other villains, it had up until then never been possible to demonstrate the connections to individually known crimes. As for the various rogues and scoundrels who did the evil work in London, although I had on occasion seen them arrested and charged, they often escaped their due punishments, because the hand of Moriarty reached out into many places, both in prisons and in the courts. But that is a digression, such as my biographer often permits himself. Let me continue with the French network. It certainly had Moriarty's mark on it. Monsieur Antoine Duvoillier was a well-known art dealer and a respected Parisian gentleman. He was the adjutant for the French network. He received from Moriarty the order to arrange the theft of the papers, and to commission their translation into German and Italian. These would then be made known to the potential purchasers. He did not of course deal with the translators directly, but through a trusted intermediary, Monsieur Jules Perrot.

"Despite my most detailed enquiries, I discovered little about Monsieur Perrot. Moreover, to my dismay I learned that my interest had been noted, and that M. Duvoillier in early February had felt obliged to find a different agent to replace M. Perrot. I did find out who this was, and his name, Monsieur Marcel Thouvenin. It seemed to me that he did not have quite the quality of his predecessor, for it was through him that I came upon the identity of both translators. The French government gave me all possible support, so that it was not difficult to effect Thouvenin's arrest by the Sûreté. On his arrest, both the originals and a translation were found. M. Thouvenin obviously realised the predicament he was in and was quite ready to assist the police. He did not reveal the names of his principals, but he was prepared to say that he had already worked on other secret papers. He also revealed that exchanges, against large sums of money, took place often in two hotels, in the Hotel de Luxembourg in Nimes, and in the Hotel Englischer Hof in Meiringen, in Switzerland.

"It was apparent that he knew more, but he hoped in revealing it that he might obtain either his freedom or a light sentence. That did not happen; M. Thouvenin was regrettably a victim of a fatal accident, in which I am sure that M. Duvoillier had a hand. With his death, the Sûreté declared that they could no longer help. The French government was clearly at this stage only too relieved at the return of the papers and wished to take no further action. I was, at a rather pompous ceremony awarded a prestigious honour, and was then, with all good wishes for a safe journey home, bound to silence. I could therefore scarcely do otherwise than to leave for London. I did however seek a contact with the translators, because I had learned their identities. A certain Henri Dumain had been invited to make an Italian translation. He however had, perhaps wisely, already left Paris, perhaps to Narbonne. I therefore took the train to Nimes, where I took a room in the illustrious Hotel de Luxembourg at the Place de l'Esplanade. To my discreet questions, I obtained no answers, as was of course only correct in such an establishment, known for its international relations, indeed, such as Professor Moriarty would cultivate.

"From Nimes I made a short trip to Narbonne, really to see if I could find M. Dumain. This however was also in vain, and I found no trace, so I occupied myself in visiting the St Just Cathedral, a most impressive structure of which the choir, as

I learned, is some 41 metres high, one of the highest in all France."

Here Holmes broke off for a moment, to fill his pipe again. I took the opportunity to mention that I had received two postcards from him, from Narbonne and from Nimes. He nodded and then continued his account.

"I returned to Nimes, took the train to Paris, and from there continued to Strasbourg. As you will know, Watson, after the Franco-Prussian War, in 1871 Strasbourg was declared the capital, within the newly united nation of Germany, of the German state of Alsace-Lorraine. From this time on Strasbourg, along with Metz and Cologne, was extensively fortified as a strongpoint of Germany's western territories. The political situation was, and remains, very complex, as a large majority of the population did not wish to be part of Germany. The economy however enjoyed a marked growth under the new conditions, and moreover the new German administration allowed for greater legislative independence than had the former centralised French government. With time, therefore, a part of the population began to accept the new conditions, and to feel more satisfied under Prussian-German rule. This was particularly the case in Strasbourg, where it clearly had applied to Herr Charles Messinger, an engineer who lived there and had been given the task of translating into German the stolen French government papers. I had the satisfaction not only of meeting Herr Messinger, but also of persuading him to shift loyalties and work with me. He agreed to work in future as my informer. I was now free to take the quickest way to London again.

"Once back in London, my first move was to send a telegram to the Reverend Horace Poultney-Jones."

I had to interrupt him here, to interject, "But that was the kind and helpful Anglican minister who resided in the summer months as chaplain to the English guests and travellers in Basle, in the Three Kings Hotel. He assisted us most valuably during our investigation of the death in Basle of the young Englishman, Charles Bradley."

"Of course, Watson", replied Holmes, who then prepared to continue. "I found it good to make contact again with Reverend Poultney-Jones, as Monsieur Thouvenin had mentioned the Hotel Englischer Hof in Meiringen. I had recalled that the minister had mentioned that his former student friend, now also an Anglican minister, had spent the summer months as an Anglican chaplain, in Meiringen, staying at the Hotel Englischer Hof. I asked Reverend Poultney-Jones for the name and address in England of his friend. He was pleased to help, and offered to accompany me to a meeting, so I found myself on a rainy morning in early April 1891, at Charing Cross station waiting for the train by which he travelled from Westerham."

I interrupted again to ask, "Westerham, in Kent?"

"Yes, Watson, Westerham is a relatively prosperous village in Kent, southeast of London. So it was that we travelled together to his old friend, taking a hansom to Liverpool Street station, and thence by local train to Sawbridgeworth." Holmes looked at me with a smile and then explained, before I could ask, that Sawbridgeworth is a village northeast of London, in Hertfordshire, and the home, since his retirement, of the Reverend George Butterford.

"The trains on the Great Eastern Railway are leisurely, but we arrived in late morning and walked up, past a water-meadow and by The Fox public house, where we turned up to the village on its small hill.

"Behind the church and vicarage, we reached our destination, Reverend Butterford's cottage. As you will readily understand, in this rustic retreat there is little diversion for a trained and educated mind. Reverend Butterford was only too pleased to welcome guests who offered an agreeable change in his daily routine. He assured us that he had heard of my supposed death before he left England in June for the 1891 season in Meiringen. We enjoyed a light lunch with him, and then I made clear the reason for my visit.

"I had regrettably to realise that both of these worthy gentlemen, for all their helpfulness, were rather loquacious. I had to lead the conversation most carefully in order to keep to that which really interested me. Believe me, it was most rewarding. Reverend Butterford assured me that there were throughout the summer many prosperous and wealthy foreigners of all types at the hotel. There were many English guests, Germans and Americans, and others included even the Italian engineers who had come to work on the Brienz-Rothorn mountain railway, then being built. With their workplace in nearby Brienz they welcomed the quiet of

Meiringen. Many travellers came to see the falls in the valley, and especially the Reichenbach Falls, or to visit the Aare Gorge.

“As he described this, which he clearly enjoyed, it was not easy to keep Reverend Butterford to the point, but finally he told me exactly that which I had been hoping to learn. At the end of September he had been mildly unwell and determined to postpone his return by a few days. There were at the end of the season no further English guests in the Hotel Englischer Hof, he therefore noted, more than he might have done, when a number of foreign gentlemen arrived on the same day, apparently always in pairs. He had no contact with them, nor did he desire it, but having at different times seen many different guests in the hotel, he formed the opinion, from their appearance and speech, that they might have been from Denmark, Germany, Italy, Russia and the Balkans.

“Reverend Butterford did however notice that these late guests were in no way interested in the sights or scenery, nor did they leave the hotel during their stay. He had the feeling that they were waiting for someone. Three days later, there arrived two further guests, and he noted that one of them spoke a very cultivated High German. Reverend Butterford felt that the others had been awaiting their arrival, On the afternoon of the same day, they all met in the reading room for a vigorous discussion, in French, a discussion which however froze when Reverend Butterford briefly passed by. As he had no wish to disturb them, and saw that all were watching him carefully, he left the reading room at once.

"The next day, the two last gentlemen to arrive had already left the hotel in the early morning, and the others dispersed during the next twenty-four hours. I asked Reverend Butterford whether he had any idea what had been discussed, but here he became somewhat embarrassed, with a sideways look to his old friend Reverend Poultney-Jones. As he explained, although he had once spoken good French, he was no longer so young, and could not always hear and remember, and he had of course in no way intended to eavesdrop. There was however one moment when he had been most surprised, for he caught the name of a mythical and evil creature, of which he had earlier heard. He had wondered how that could feature in the visitors' discussion. I must have looked particularly curious, because he insisted that he had remembered correctly, and that it was to the 'basilisk' that they had referred.

"He had left the hotel for England shortly afterwards and knew no more. The great Meiringen fire destroyed much of the town in that autumn, not long after he left, and since there would scarcely be guests now, he resolved not to return there again, but remain in future in his cottage."

Here Holmes stopped his account briefly, and then looked questioningly at me. I could not follow his thoughts however, and so he continued,

"Reverend Butterford was naturally in error as he feared that the company was discussing fabulous and mythical creatures, and in particular the basilisk, of which popular superstition said that just to look upon it would lead to instant death. No,

Watson, they had discussed something just as deadly, not at all a legend but the new torpedo-boat 'Basilisk II.' You and I had learned of this during our enquiries into Charles Bradley's death in Switzerland in Basle in autumn 1890. It is a curious chance that just in Basle, where Bradley had died, the basilisk is a well-known legendary feature of the city. I was able subsequently to confirm, with brother Mycroft, from his position in our government, that plans of the torpedo-boat of that name were known to be circulating in Germany, but also in Denmark, Italy and Russia. Mr. Butterford had now confirmed that Meiringen was involved in the exchange of secret material."

As my friend lifted his whisky glass, I used the opportunity to ask a question that had troubled me. I had read of the Meiringen fire in autumn 1891, but this was urgent.

"Holmes, can you in any way suggest who the men might be, on whom, in Reverend Butterford's view, the other parties had been waiting?"

"Yes, Watson, for it is clear that such affairs were in the hands of highly placed persons of confidence in Professor Moriarty's criminal network. The handing over of sensitive secret papers, and of the large sums which change hands for such information, demanded this. I believe therefore that one of the two men was the French adjutant, Monsieur Duvoillier. The other I do not know by name, but as Reverend Butterford said that he spoke an excellent and cultivated High German, as well as French, I was at once sure that we had already encountered him, in autumn 1890 in Basle."

He waited, and I looked at him again a little irritated. "Yes," he said, "He is that man who was always in the background, to whom the local agents only referred by his pseudonym, the 'German Knife-Grinder,' as you will recall".

My reaction was one of complete incredulity. "The German Knife-Grinder? That can surely not be! Yes, I know our enquiries into the mysterious death of the Englishman Charles Bradley in Basle led us unexpectedly to the trail of this man, but we never even saw him, let alone learnt anything about him. We had no doubt that he was in Professor Moriarty's service, but surely only as one of the working agents."

Holmes reflected carefully before speaking again.

"Deception and disguise seem to be second nature to this man. He was certainly not just another agent. He was in charge and represented Moriarty. He is obviously a master of concealment. Choosing the character of a knife-grinder, a typical task for an old soldier, was brilliant; it gave him all the freedom he required, to appear anywhere and to enter any house. Watson, without going into detail, I was already convinced that when we were there, and only by hearsay, we encountered a person with as many facets as the finest polished diamond. I knew we would hear of him again."

He stopped and looked again at his whisky glass.

Sherlock Holmes' Plan

I found the account which Holmes had given me so far completely absorbing, although I admit to some reticence about the German Knife-Grinder, as I could not entirely follow his reasoning. I knew however that it was my privilege to hear these events, now some time behind us, because of our deep and trusting friendship. I had however still not really understood why our departure in haste from London in April 1891 had not been a flight from Moriarty. But before I could come to grips with this, Holmes had started again, with an apparently abstruse question in no way associated with that which I had heard.

"Watson, do you recognise the name of Hiram Stevens Maxim?"

"I think I may have seen it in the newspapers, but I do not know in what connection."

"Allow me, then, to refresh your memory, old friend. Mr. Maxim is a native of the New World and is known as an inventor of a variety of mechanisms and products. He seems to have succeeded in inventing a completely new type of gun, which can fire at least five hundred rounds per minute."

"You mean then Holmes, a kind of repeating weapon, such as they had at the end of the American Civil War?"

"No, Watson, that was a weapon which Mr. Maxim seems to have developed much further. At that time the principle was to feed the ammunition into the weapon as regularly as possible, with a manually worked handle. Mr. Maxim's weapon uses the recoil to reject the empty case and feed in the next cartridge, and the ammunition is led into the weapon in a continuous textile band, which passes through the mechanism. The acute overheating which such weapons suffered was relieved in the past by allowing several barrels to rotate in a cylinder, each barrel firing one shot in turn, and being cooled, often inadequately, by air. Maxim's gun is cooled more effectively by a water reservoir."

All this was of interest, and I did recall reading of it at some time past, but Holmes was anxious to go further.

"Let us now study Mr. Maxim. He moved to London in the early 1880s, setting up a workshop in Holborn. He was able to test and demonstrate his new weapon at that time and even demonstrate it in public. He continued to seek to improve it and has obviously had some success. In April 1891, however, a set of plans and drawings of his most recent model, for a much improved and lighter model of his weapon, were stolen. This fact was not made public, but I learned of it from Mycroft, who asked me to investigate. As I began discreetly to make enquiries, the suspicion grew, that Professor Moriarty had his hand in the matter. If that were so, then the plans would certainly have gone at the earliest opportunity to the continent. Enquiries with the Sûreté, however, who are normally most helpful, assured me that M. Duvoillier had not left Paris. This news surprised me because in such an important affair he, as Moriarty's adjutant in France, was the obvious person to undertake the task. I then learned however that he could indeed not have been travelling, as he was in hospital with an acute attack of appendicitis, and his condition was critical."

I interrupted Holmes here as a doctor, to say to him, "Indeed, an inflammation of the appendix is always serious and must be treated with great care. If there is, as easily happens, a rupture, then the patient's chances of recovery are small."

Holmes followed my comment carefully, but did not make a remark, going on to say,

"I suspected that, in such circumstances, Colonel Sebastian Moran might be the most likely to be called on, to take on the task that M. Duvoillier would have left unfinished. It was not long before my enquiries were rewarded; I also received a coded message from my informant in Strasbourg, M. Messinger, confirming my suspicion.

"M. Messinger also told me that an Englishman and a German had arranged a meeting with him, to ascertain whether he could produce translations into German of a number of stolen secret documents, descriptions of a secret automatic weapon."

This provoked my next question. "Is M. Messinger then able to make adequate translations into German from English as he can from French?"

"No," replied Holmes. "And I did not suggest to you that he could. His knowledge of English is competent, but certainly not at the level necessary for the task being discussed. His command of French is, however, excellent, and as a trained engineer he had obtained the necessary skills to reproduce the drawings with all necessary precision".

Holmes paused again and drew on his pipe. "He was now awaiting a French translation of the stolen papers, which should be brought to him. In the meantime, it was intended that Colonel Moran should take over the functions in Moriarty's network of Monsieur Duvoillier, acutely ill in hospital.

"As this became apparent, I came to a conviction that this might at long last be the opportunity to make fast Professor Moriarty. Following my success earlier of securing the French secret governmental papers, I hoped that a certain goodwill and support would be forthcoming. I was able, with the aid of a constructed story, to arrange that Colonel Moran was charged and, for the period up to a court case, would be detained in custody in France. This obliged Professor Moriarty to intervene, if he were not to miss the opportunity of selling the stolen plans. His decision to travel to Paris himself, and to lead to a conclusion the work which Colonel Moran had already started, was perhaps all the easier, as he knew that just at that moment I was on the point of destroying his network in London. Being however a most intelligent opponent, he visited me in Baker Street to ascertain whether I was in some way connected with Colonel Moran's arrest in France. He naturally would not ask me directly, but led a cat and mouse game around me, a game that I resisted. He left me without learning anything."

“Even so, Holmes, he threatened you, and there were several incidents afterwards,” I remarked.

“Yes, Watson, it is certainly true that he carefully but unmistakeably threatened me. And as you say, there were subsequently incidents which supported his threats, including starting a fire in these rooms. But all these apparent attacks, directly threatening as they may have appeared, were still meant only to be a warning to me. The order to murder me had not yet been given. Believe me, old friend, if he had wanted to have me killed, he would have had it done.”

I was appalled to hear this from my friend, which, as he was recounting it in such a calm manner, seemed to him to be as natural as when he stopped again to fill his pipe. A moment later he was speaking again.

“It was of course my intention that Professor Moriarty should believe that I took his warning seriously. I had to deceive him. He must think that I would leave London, and at least be absent while the police were attempting to arrest the members of his network.

“I have a certain preference for Sussex, as you, and your readers, and others, already know. This was, I was sure, also known to Professor Moriarty, so that should I depart towards the south, it would only confirm him in his hope that I was leaving London. As long as he felt that I represented no danger to his plans for the stolen weapons documents in France, I was sure that he would act as I hoped, and intended, he should.

"It all seemed to be going well. I had already learned then that Professor Moriarty had ordered a special train for the afternoon of April 25. This information came through the Baker Street Irregulars. Those street lads had once again shown me, as so often in the past, how truly valuable they could be. But now, our departure: This was also an urgent matter, as I wanted make certain Moriarty truly believed, as he left for France, that his threats and the warning actions had had the desired effect. He should believe that, as I valued my life, I had gone away to hide. Since he was a very intelligent and very dangerous opponent, I took some special measures to show him that I really was fleeing from him. That is why I called on you that evening, on April 24, as I felt that if you were to accompany me, that would surely be seen as proof of your helping me when I was in mortal danger."

As he recounted this story, he again stopped, leaving an uncomfortable silence hanging in the room. I was slowly beginning to understand that our departure from London really was no flight, but I was still troubled that all this had been concealed from me. Why had he not trusted me? I had kept so many secrets and confidences with him, and so, why not this?

His next words answered my unspoken question.

"I truly could not tell you what my intentions were. You would have inevitably behaved differently, however you might have tried. You do not have the necessary theatrical skills, or indeed, the nature, to live a deception. But I have already made clear to you that the whole action needed to be completely convincing, if it were to succeed."

Holmes had with these words already calmed my first reactions, but I was still not satisfied.

"But once we had left London, might you not then have taken me into your confidence?"

He reflected for a moment before replying. "One might think so today, but I had at the time the most convincing reasons to behave as I did. Perhaps it will be best if I tell you now the rest of the story, so that you may form your own opinion.

"As our train left Victoria, I was admittedly surprised to see Professor Moriarty there. I had not thought that as he was going to the ferry in Dover, his special train would be following quite so closely behind the regular Continental Express to Dover on which we were travelling. That surely would however further puzzle him, for we would not take that train to go to Sussex. I let it be a help, however, to introduce another indication that we were truly running from him. Remember how we left the train at Canterbury, leaving our registered baggage to go on to Dover and Paris. In this way we obtained distance from Moriarty, and encouraged him, the Napoleon of crime, again to believe that we were truly anxious to escape from him, and certainly not to follow him to France. He would have had no more suspicion, at least as long as we behaved cleverly.

"Let us however think of Canterbury. After Professor Moriarty's special train had gone through, we had to find out how to travel to Newhaven, where we arrived in time to take a late ferry to Dieppe. From that port, as you may recall, the trains do not go to the Gare du Nord in Paris, but to the Gare St. Lazare, the station which serves the west coast of France. Moriarty, if he had believed we were indeed on the way to Paris, certainly had his agents at the Gare du Nord to observe the arrivals. My caution in this respect led me to break our journey at the Hotel Terminus adjacent to St. Lazare. We could rest there, and early next morning a cab brought us inconspicuously to the Gare du Nord, so that we could take a morning express from there to Brussels."

Holmes made here another short pause, and then asked me, "You surely recall the Hotel de Belle-Vue in Brussels?"

I did, of course, and somewhat irritated I replied, "Naturally, Holmes, such a noble establishment is not easily forgotten. The guestbook shows that almost all the Royal households of Europe had stayed there. I recall that the hotel porter told me that even Wellington, as he collected together his general staff before Waterloo, spent some nights there, but…"

My story was clearly out of place, for Holmes interrupted me sharply, and continued his narrative.

"Watson, I meant the situation of the hotel. On the opposite side of the road is the Hotel de Flandres. Some years ago, when you were not yet at my side, I was called to Brussels to clear up a case of theft. I discovered that that the two hotels are connected by an underground passage. I took advantage of this on our second day in Brussels, after you had gone to bed, to meet there an agent of my brother, Mycroft. This had been arranged before we left London. Mycroft's agent had learned from my Strasbourg informer, Mr. Messinger, that Professor Moriarty had indeed taken over, at short notice, the task of Colonel Moran. It was planned that the exchange of plans and money should take place at the Hotel Englischer Hof in Meiringen in the Bernese Oberland. Some of those who had an interest in the sale of the stolen papers would, however, even if they took trains like the Orient Express, need three or more days to reach Meiringen at this time of year. It had apparently therefore been decided that the delegates should arrive in Meiringen at the latest on May 3rd.

"The delay, together with the waiting which would be involved before my trap could be sprung, was naturally disagreeable. There was however another more serious matter. It was not at all certain that we would have the support of the Swiss authorities; and without this we could not rely upon the police in Canton Berne, in which Meiringen lies. Mycroft had already in London warned me that his authority had its limits. Switzerland, as a neutral country, which has had its constitution only since 1848, is in principle opposed to, and very cautious about, any attempt by foreigners to interfere in its internal affairs. The separate cantons also jealously guard their own historical competences. Mycroft's agent told me that I would very soon learn whether Mycroft's diplomatic efforts had borne fruit. I told this agent that we would the next day leave Brussels for Strasbourg, to stay there at the Grand

Hotel Ville de Paris, and that I could then be reached by telegram until further notice."

As Holmes paused again in his account, to draw thoughtfully on his pipe, I remembered an incident. "While we were in the hotel in Strasbourg you did indeed have a telegram from the police in London, but I do not recall one from your brother."

Holmes allowed himself an amused smile. "My friend, you are quite right. There was a telegram. Can you remember now, as you recall so well the incident, what happened then?"

I did not have to think long, as so many details of that journey were etched indelibly in my memory. "You read the telegram. You then told me that they had rounded up almost all the band members in Moriarty's network, but that Professor Moriarty and his adjutant Colonel Moran had escaped. In frustration you screwed up the telegram and threw it into the fire."

"Brilliant, Watson. Your memory is in the best of condition! But now I must ask you to think about what I already told you this evening. Why should it have annoyed me to learn that Moriarty and Moran had escaped, when I already knew that Moriarty had left London for Paris? And when I also knew that Colonel Moran was sitting in a French prison? I knew quite well that Moriarty was on his way to Paris to arrange the sale of the secret papers."

As I followed his words, he looked at me challengingly.

"Holmes, you are quite right, it really did not make sense." Suddenly I saw that the truth was quite different. "That telegram was from your brother Mycroft!"

"Excellent, Watson. It told me clearly that I could expect no help from the Swiss authorities. Moreover, because there had already been a diplomatic incident in Geneva involving one of their agents, the British government would certainly, if challenged, refuse to acknowledge any responsibility for my actions in Switzerland. You will certainly recall, Watson, that I had repeatedly assured you that I would willingly sacrifice my own life, if I knew that we would thereby free the world of Professor Moriarty, the embodiment of evil. I was not therefore deterred by Mycroft's message.

"I could naturally not know what would in fact take place," he continued, "but it was quite certain that there must at some stage be a confrontation. Since I did not wish to burden you with this dilemma, I told you that the telegram was from the London police, and to ensure that you did not see it, I threw it in the fire. Since, however, I also could not consider exposing you to the dangers which would certainly await us in Meiringen, I tried to convince you that you should travel back to London. That was a mistake, for which I must reproach myself."

He smiled and took another draft of whisky.

The Reichenbach Falls

I was, I admit, at this very late hour, somewhat dazed by all I had heard, and also over his severe judgment of himself. My face revealed my question.

"When I suggested that you should now travel home, as with me you would be in danger, I achieved the opposite result. You have always been my most faithful and loyal friend, and I should have known that your immediate reaction would be to declare that you would not leave me alone in a dangerous situation. In all the years where we had worked together, you had always been true. And here we were on a Monday afternoon in Strasbourg and I made the unforgiveable mistake of ignoring this. I was asking you to leave me alone to face the dangers. I fear that Mycroft's telegram had disturbed my judgment. I thus ignored one of my fundamental principles, not to be swayed by emotion."

My friend's words touched my heart. My earlier annoyance at not knowing from the start what we were trying to achieve, as he had not taken me into his confidence, had already subsided. This however was different. I had seen that the time had come, where I should express openly my forgiveness for doubting him, and that I had forgiven his necessary secrecy. Holmes kept his feelings carefully under control, and some might say that he had no feelings, but I knew from his change of manner, that he was as moved as I was. For a few moments all was silent, and then he continued, in a quiet but clear voice, his extraordinary story.

"As you will remember, we left Strasbourg on Monday afternoon and travelled via Basle to Geneva. We then travelled up the Rhône valley, arriving finally at a small town called Leuk. There we engaged a mountain guide, who told us, before our next stage, about the history and significance of Leuk, a trading centre of ancient times, and of the path we were now to follow. Traders, merchants, soldiers, officials of church and government, and today many tourists, took the path here, a historic mule track, between the Valais and the Bernese Oberland. This trail, known for centuries, is the Gemmi Pass. It climbs first from Leuk steeply up a cliff face to reach a high valley with a good path to the north. Admittedly, it may appear an adventurous way to arrive later at Interlaken, but we had time. Our guide however told us that the winter of 1890-1891 had been the most severe in living memory, and there were still large amounts of snow making the path more laborious. Do you recall, Watson, how he had told us that the Alpnach Lake, in fact an arm of Lake Lucerne, had been hard frozen for four months?"

As I nodded, I recalled an incident. "Holmes, I remember that, after we had reached the cliff top above Leuk and were on the trail along the melancholy Dauben Lake, a large rock fell from the cliff above, into the lake behind us. Your behaviour led me to feel that you thought it was no accident, but an attempt to harm us. Surely, however, in view of what you have told me, that could not be?"

"Correct, Watson. Our guide said that happened a lot at that time of year, and I am sure he was right. I found it a useful moment to underline that we were threatened at all times. If we were in danger, we must at all times be vigilant, and this, together with the arduous trail over the pass, the snow, and your leg, irreparably wounded in Afghanistan, might persuade you that the time had come to let me continue alone to Meiringen. I had of course again underestimated the endurance of an old soldier, and the loyalty of a real friend."

"Should that tell me that the only purpose of this mountain tour in the snow was to persuade me to give up?"

"Of course not, Watson. My first concern was, not in any way to be observed on the way, for we had to prevent Professor Moriarty from learning even indirectly that we might be here. A mountain tour seemed to me a most appropriate occupation. In respect of yourself, I would certainly have been relieved if you had chosen not to accompany me any further. As it was, we reached Meiringen exactly as I had planned on the 3rd, May. We took our rooms in the Hotel Englischer Hof, which was then managed by Peter Steiler the Elder. My study of the guestbook and my observations at dinner in the dining-room confirmed my expectation that Professor Moriarty's clients were already in attendance. They did not know me, nor I them, but it was clear that they were not tourists. Moriarty himself was not there, so he had either chosen to stay elsewhere, or had not yet arrived.

I interrupted Holmes to ask, "The clients of whom you speak: Were they always in pairs, from each country? And if so, why should that be?"

“Indeed they were, Watson, also on this occasion, and the reason is really quite clear. One of the two is a leading military expert and must be able to judge the value to his country’s army of the product being offered. The other has the authority to make the agreed payments. You will understand that in such transactions very substantial sums of money are involved. I must admit that despite a most searching investigation, I have not yet found out how such payments are actually realised. I only know that, whenever such sales of secret papers are involved, there are two leading members of Professor Moriarty’s criminal network involved. The procedure seems to be that the purchaser sees a part of the papers, but not all. Once an interest has been established, the payment has to be made. One of Moriarty’s representatives then goes to the point agreed for the payment, and when the full amount is received, sends a telegram to the second representative, that is, Moriarty’s adjutant, to confirm the full payment. Only then are the remaining papers released to the buyer.”

I had here of course to ask the obvious question: “What if the payment is not made as agreed? The purchaser might depart with part of the papers in his hand.”

“I believe that the extract first offered is perhaps a sample of the whole, interesting enough to lead to purchase, but so incomplete as to be useless alone.”

“And can it occur that on learning that the money has been paid, the representative of Moriarty simply leaves without handing over the papers?”

"He would, quite simply, not live long. First, not to act in accordance with Moriarty's instructions is a fatal mistake. Much worse, however, is the risk of angering the client. These are not cheap criminals, but leading state officials, often quite unscrupulous, usually corrupt, and with enormous influence in many quarters – I will shortly come back to this. First, however, please let me continue with the chronological account of events. As it became clear on the morning of May the 4th that Professor Moriarty was not yet in Meiringen, it seemed advisable to spend the night away from the Hotel. With Peter Steiler's advice, I decided to stay one night in the hotel at Rosenlaui, up the valley. Peter Steiler told me that there would be snow. The hotel was not yet opened for the season, but the staff from Meiringen might be there, airing and cleaning the rooms before the opening later in May.

"He told us that he could not be sure, but that if this were so, they would certainly find us a place to spend the night. Should Rosenlaui, however, not yet be open or the snow too deep, we could turn back, and after a three-hour walk down, still be back for dinner in Meiringen. He also urged us not to miss the few minutes' detour from the mule track, to see the spectacular Falls of the Reichenbach, one of the great wonders of the district. We followed this good advice and set off after an early lunch."

Holmes had to pause again, and we were both obviously led in our thoughts to remember that walk and its consequences. It is indeed a fearful place and has left such a vivid memory that even now, many years later, I recall all the details.

"You will remember the village lad who brought us a note as we were at the falls?"

"I do indeed, Holmes, and can never forget. It carried the stamp of our hotel, and the proprietor had written that an English lady had arrived, on the way to Lucerne, dying of consumption, and had suffered a dangerous outbreak of bleeding. Herr Steiler begged me to come back to see her, as the lady would not allow a Swiss doctor to treat her. I had of course to respect such a request, and so left you alone. It was about an hour's walk down to the hotel. Only on enquiry in the hotel, where they knew nothing about it, did I realise that the letter was a fiction. Shaking with fear, I turned and set off again to the Falls, but I needed two hours up the steep path. There was no trace of you, but, observing as you had taught me, I deduced that there had been a fight. It was clear from the marks on the path that you must both have fallen into the ravine."

I had to draw breath to calm down, but asked Holmes, "You left me a long note, several pages, in which you told me you knew the letter was fraudulent. Was that really so, or had you only suspected it?"

"No, Watson," he continued, "it was a certainty, and was at once obvious, given my knowledge of the geography and rail system of Switzerland. I knew that at the end of April very few, and least of all one so seriously ill, could traverse the high mountain passes, with their deep snow. And remember that we had been told that the Swiss winter of 1890-1891 was of an all-time severity. If, as the letter claimed, the lady was on her way from Davos to Lucerne, the only way was by train via Zürich and directly to Lucerne. Meiringen would not have been even on the way, nor feasible, and so not even a place to lodge for a night. The letter was therefore on sight a complete deception, but it meant that you had to go back to help a dying Englishwoman, and you left me there. You were barely out of sight and calling distance when Professor Moriarty appeared. To my surprise he proposed that, if I still valued my life, I give him at once the second half of the stolen secret papers.

"I knew nothing of this, and so was unprepared for such a challenge, but did not let him see that. I let him think that I would consider his demand. At the same time, I asked him, making my mistrust of his offer the reason, to allow me time to write a few lines to you, my old friend. This he agreed with a malevolent smile, and I wrote my note, laid it on a stone, and so weighed it down with my cigarette case and my alpenstock, that I was sure you would find it."

He paused and played thoughtfully with his whisky glass.

"Dear Holmes, in the time when I and the whole world thought you were dead, those pages with your last words to me were a treasured souvenir," I told him.

The room suddenly again seemed to go very quiet.

I had however a question.

"Now that I have heard your earlier explanations, I can understand what Professor Moriarty had in mind, when he asked about the whereabouts of the second half of the secret plans; but what did that mean?"

"There, Watson, I can only speculate. It seems probable to me that there may also have been the documents which Moriarty took when he left London, enabling him to rebuild his own criminal network."

I looked at Holmes in some puzzlement.

"You will understand that as I explained to you. I had been able to achieve the end of the network in London. The police had arrested the persons involved. These were however only the operative members of the band, those who carried out the individual acts within his empire. The really important persons in key positions, such as corrupt or blackmailed lawyers, judges or police, could not be touched. As long as Moriarty had the means of reaching these persons in future, such as by possession of debt and loan pledges, promissory notes, or other compromising documents, he could at once start to reconstruct his network."

That seemed clear to me. And so I asked, "But without these papers he was then unable to act?"

"Quite so, Watson."

"But do you then have an idea where they now might be?"

"There we are in a completely hypothetical field, Watson.

"I had suspected that Professor Moriarty's partner, who had left Meiringen as soon as the first part of the secret papers had been handed over, had taken the second part of the papers with him. I suggested to Moriarty that this was so, but he considered this idea unacceptable and impossible. He did say that his partner had departed without baggage, and that he could not have concealed the papers in his travelling clothes. Perhaps more significant, he assured me of his complete trust in the unwavering loyalty of this partner, a man of honour, about whom he had not the least doubt. As I suggested that I, who did not know who this person might be, was not so easily convinced, he allowed himself an indiscretion. Moriarty told me that I had already had opportunity, during my investigations in Basle into Charles Bradley's death, to observe the efficient and unscrupulous manner in which his partner carried out his tasks."

I could not restrain my outburst. "Then we must be talking again of the German Knife-Grinder, whom we did not meet when we were in Basle, but who was always there in the background! You suspected already then a link to Moriarty, and Reverend Butterford seems to have seen him later again in Meiringen."

"Quite, Watson, and yet, despite the praise which Moriarty accorded him, I am still convinced that he is the one who has stolen the papers, and concealed them, perhaps somewhere in Meiringen, as he did not risk being seen with them on leaving. The German Knife-Grinder is a very clever one. We do not know who he is, but he has certainly recognised that Professor Moriarty's London network is for the moment destroyed. That in France is also temporarily ineffective. If, as I suspect, he realised the power that Moriarty's papers could confer, he has not hesitated to act. Moreover, if he has the second part of the secret papers, he may even be preparing to sell this at his own price, for example to the Imperial German Government."

At this point Holmes hesitated in his suspicions, and I suggested, "If your hypothesis is correct, then he may have found a hiding place not far from the Hotel Englischer Hof."

"I thought so too, Watson, and as I had learned that Moriarty had lodged in the Hotel Victoria, my brother sent an agent, not long after you had returned to Britain, to search for the possible hiding place. This was however unsuccessful."

"Perhaps the German Knife-Grinder got there first?"

"That is quite possible, but I now suspect rather that he wished to allow time for Meiringen to calm down, before he appeared there again. There was much less risk of being recognised, or attracting attention, when our fatal Reichenbach Falls incident was no longer the talk of the village. At that time, I thought a careful and thorough search after the season might be the most useful approach. Regrettably, that never happened."

"And why not?"

"Because Meiringen was, as you recall, largely destroyed on October 25th, 1891 in the fire to which Reverend Butterworth had referred. Investigation showed that it started early in the morning, and with the strong Föhn wind for which the region is well known, the fire spread rapidly west through the wooden buildings forming the town. Of many buildings, only ruins remained, such as the chimneys of the Hotel Victoria."

I had to ask the obvious question: "And what happened to the people there?"

"Most lost all they had, but all seem to have survived, save one very old man, blind and living alone."

"And what became of our friendly host, Herr Steiler, and his Englischer Hof?"

"The Föhn wind, this warm, dry Alpine wind so well known in those parts, determined the direction taken by the flames. The more southerly part of the town survived, and with it the Englischer Hof, the railway station and its workshops.

"But let me now continue with the chronological sequence of events at the Reichenbach Falls. When Moriarty asked me again what I had done with his papers, I answered truthfully, that, if he had lost them, I was certainly not the thief. He shouted and argued, as I told you. Suddenly, however, he launched himself upon me. Professor Moriarty, whom I had up to now known only as a cold-blooded and refined strategic thinker, hurled himself in a wild rage at me. Without that knowledge of Japanese Baritsu wrestling which has more than once been an invaluable help, I must have fallen with him into the abyss below."

"Holmes, it really was in no way the image of Professor Moriarty which I had retained, after so many conversations with you."

"Exactly; I can only agree with you, Watson. I suspect that his behaviour was prompted not only by the alleged theft, but by the knowledge that the second part of the secret papers was also gone. Fear possessed him; for he could not now deliver on his promise, when the payment for purchase of the papers was complete. That was fatal. As I told you, such deals, with such clients, permit no failures. Professor Moriarty knew this all too well. In the desperate conviction that I knew what had happened, that I might even be in possession of the missing items, he had come to confront me. We will never know whether he believed me. It is not even important, as he really already knew that his position was hopeless. The mask of the cold strategist fell away. He had, as a gambler, pitted his whole intellect against me. I believe that it was, in this last and greatest battle of wits, the realisation, that he had gambled and lost, which he could no longer hold under control."

I nodded and hoped Holmes would tell me what now led into his disappearance. I was not to be disappointed, for he continued at once.

"I had narrowly escaped death. I realised at once, however, that the Bernese and Swiss authorities could now at once charge me with murder or manslaughter."

"Come, Holmes, they would scarcely do that with a man of your reputation and integrity."

"Do not believe it, Watson. For the Swiss authorities, all they would know, if I reappeared, was that two foreign visitors had gone to the falls and had had an argument on the path, and that one of them had fallen to his death. Those are most suspicious circumstances. You will moreover remember that Mycroft expressly warned me that I could expect no support from the British government. Equally, however, it occurred to me that it might be more than useful, if those criminals whom I had not yet laid low, could be told that I no longer lived. These thoughts inspired me to my next moves. I examined the rock face above me, and saw that although a mistake might be fatal, I could take this last risk and climb up. It was a most unpleasant and laborious matter, Watson, and I was more than relieved to reach a small ledge on which I could rest and observe. I was lying there, drawing breath again, as you, my dear Watson, appeared."

He continued.

"You saw, as I had hoped, the tracks we had made on the wet path, you found the message which I had left for you, and you told the two policemen who accompanied you, and others who had made the climb, of your conclusion, that Professor Moriarty and I must have fallen together into the abyss of the Falls. I was surprised that there were a number of other men with you. It seemed clear that Herr Steiler, our most helpful host at the Englischer Hof, had organised support. After your return and the discovery that the letter was a deception, he would certainly have considered it necessary to call the police, and so summoned a group of followers to accompany you.

When all left again for Meiringen, I could consider leaving my hiding place

I had barely stretched my legs, when a great boulder rolled down from the cliff above. I was most surprised to see, briefly but clearly, the face of Colonel Moran. He had apparently been released from the French prison sooner than I thought and had at once found the way to Meiringen to follow Moriarty. I could lose no time, for I must escape from the ledge. My descent to the path was more a slide than a climb down, but despite dirty and torn clothes, and several bleeding wounds, I reached the path and found my way out before Moran found me again. I was anxious to put as much distance as possible between us. I also knew now that Moran was aware that I had survived. I considered however that he would say nothing, because his own link with Moriarty would come out. That might be fatal.

"Now I could see how precarious my situation was. I could not risk being discovered or recognised. That excluded my going back to Meiringen. My only option seemed to be the mule track, which led up to the Reichenbach valley and away from the falls, up towards Rosenlaui. I knew that this way would lead ultimately to Grindelwald, but what the conditions in late winter might be I knew not at all. It was now already getting dark. Progress was hard, and I was exhausted, cold, hungry, and had several injuries. I would have to find somewhere to rest. Above the Zwirgi Inn, there are several clearings with Alpine meadows, with various wooden huts. Most were empty, as they served in the summer for cheesemaking on these meadows.

Fortunately, in just one of these I saw a faint yellow light. I knocked on the heavy wooden door and found an old, certainly very poor but most hospitable dairyman. He asked no questions, and I could hardly understand a word of his dialect, but for a few coins he offered me fresh spring water, a piece of hard bread, and some of his cheese. And for the night he showed me where I could sleep in his dry hayloft, I tried to show my gratitude, but for him it was self-evident to help a traveller. Before falling into a deep sleep, I took stock of my position.

"It was certainly my intention to leave Switzerland as soon as possible, but that was clearly not easy. Where should I go? My clothing was torn and dishevelled, I was injured and rather dirty, and as an English-speaking traveller in that condition, I would certainly attract suspicion. Adding to the problem was that most of my money, my papers and rail tickets were down at the Englischer Hof and could not now be touched. I had only a few francs in my pocket, which had been intended for a night at the Rosenlaui Hotel.

He paused to summarise.

"To leave Switzerland I would need a completely new start with new papers, a new name, and adequate money. For this I had only one person to whom I could go, my brother, Mycroft. My aim must therefore be, once over the hill to Grindelwald, and then to travel inconspicuously to Berne where is situated the British Embassy, so as to reach Mycroft by diplomatic channels. He might have of course to disown me, but I saw no other possibility. I went to sleep turning this idea over. I woke in the early morning, to see the hills lit up by the rising sun. I washed myself in the water trough. I breakfasted again with my host, a delightful man, and then took my way, with a little advice, to walk to Grindelwald. This would be exactly ten miles over the mountain, from the falls.

"On the way I saw the Rosenlaui Hotel, which was, as I had been warned, still boarded and shuttered at the end of a hard winter. I seemed to be the only person here. The mule track led on uphill, not too steeply, and where animals had been driven over, the snow was pressed down. In mid-morning I was on the pass of the Grosse Scheidegg, and from there the path led in zigzags down to Grindelwald. I had learned earlier that there was since last year a new rail line from Grindelwald to Interlaken. But first I had to descend to the village. The first part of the descent is steep, but as soon as I reached the upper part of the village, it was much easier. I was however so exhausted, that the ten miles over the mountain from the falls felt like double that distance.

I looked at him and thought of the ordeal.

He went on.

"As I walked down through the village, I noticed the church used for Anglican worship, one of the many in the Swiss mountains, and for a moment hoped that I might find an upright and trustworthy person to help me. It was not so; all was closed, and a notice told me the minister would only arrive at the start of the season in June. There were few visitors on this May 5th, in the snow; all was quiet, but I bought bread at a small baker's shop, and continued down the street. I looked therefore for the newly built station, which is at the bottom of the village street. The timetable displayed showed that there were only two trains daily to Interlaken in this quiet season, so I resolved to take the 3.25 p.m. train and to travel third class, which cost me three francs and fifty cents. My remaining funds were diminishing, but third class, on the bare wooden seat of the austere wagon, was certainly, given my appearance, a better place to be. There were in any case few passengers. At half past five I reached Interlaken. I had earlier seen in my Baedeker that there was no British consul, but at least a long-established Anglican church with a resident churchwarden, who also cared for the church and its affairs in the wintertime.

"At the station there was an information board with addresses for visitors. The Anglican church and its churchwarden were listed. I walked there in fifteen minutes and could scarcely go wrong, as it was in part of the former monastery, to which the way was signposted. I knocked on the door of the churchwarden and took him at once into my confidence to ask for his help. He knew my name! Without hesitating, he welcomed me, offered warm water and clean clothes, and arranged to send a telegram to the British ambassador in Berne. I included in this a coded message for Mycroft in London. A little later, during a satisfying dinner, there arrived a telegram from the minister telling me to travel the next morning to Berne, including all instructions. Clean and warm, I slept soundly in a soft bed again, and at 9.20 next morning, was already on the way to Berne.

"It was not then an easy journey. The first local train took me to Därligen, on the lake, and from there we had a ferry to Thun. There then followed another train. Arriving punctually in Berne at a quarter to one, I found, as instructed, that an embassy official awaited me with a private carriage, to take me to the embassy in Feldeggweg, overlooking the river. I was just in time, for the news of the struggle and deaths at the Reichenbach Falls were that day in the newspapers.

"Over lunch, the minister showed me Mycroft's telegram. This assured me that in the next two days I would receive letters of credit, and that a set of papers, giving me a new identity, would be sent by courier, in the daily diplomatic bag.

"Holmes, wonderful, you were now safe!"

"Not quite, Watson, there was a lot to do. I now spent three quiet days as a guest at the embassy. During this time, I bought baggage and new clothes, while various confidential exchanges described to me the task Mycroft expected me now to undertake, as his agent. This was a perfect realisation of my wish to disappear, both from Switzerland and from my old life, and I gladly agreed. So it was that early on May 10th, I took the train shortly after six o'clock to Lucerne, from where I had a through booking to Milan on the morning Gotthard Railway express. I arrived there at 7.30 that evening, already at home in my new identity. The next morning, I continued my journey to Florence, the first destination in Mycroft's plans. It was an extraordinary thought, that only one week earlier, I had been in a fight to the death at the Reichenbach

Falls. Now, however, I could set it all aside and dedicate myself to the task before me, which I am pleased to say, proved entirely worthy of my capabilities.

“At this point, my dear Watson, I must tell you that everything that I then did falls under a curtain of complete discretion and secrecy, for which I have given my word of honour. I can tell you no more.”

Holmes had ended his account. It was very quiet, as each of us reflected on it all.

Suddenly Holmes looked and said, “Watson, I think it really is time to go to bed.” My pocket-watch showed me that it was indeed long after midnight. I suddenly felt a leaden tiredness, which surely resulted from the late hour, the generous whisky, and the total concentration which Holmes’ account had demanded.

“Indeed, I am very tired, Holmes,” I said.

He smiled and reassured me. “Mrs. Hudson has prepared the bed in your old room as new, so that you will surely have a good night. Now sleep well.”

“Thank you, Holmes, I wish you also a good night.” I almost stumbled on my way, but as soon as I lay down, went soundly to sleep.

The Crystal Palace in Sydenham

Even so, I had dreamed of some of the episodes in Holmes' account. I felt a heavy hand on my shoulder, and thought it was my dream, but no, it was someone shaking me, to awaken me. I was alarmed and reached instinctively to light my candle beside the bed, but that was not needed; it was Holmes, already dressed, beside my bed.

"Wake up, Watson, time is pressing!" Holmes' voice tolerated no contradiction.

I blinked and struggled to think clearly. "What time is it?"

"It's just after five o'clock."

"What?" I asked incredulously, and then I had a thought. "Is something burning?"

"My dear old friend, we have to hurry, Inspector Gregson has been so kind as to inform me of a crime during the night. I will explain it all on the way."

Holmes was already leaving my bedroom. "On the way?" I called out, rather confused.

"We have to take the train to Sydenham, and now please hurry, because there is a train at six-twenty from London Bridge station."

One consequence of my military service is that I can move and prepare quickly and correctly when the need is present. Holmes had already found a free hansom, and promised the driver a generous tip, when we arrived in time for the train. He set off at an alarming pace, for a hair-raising gallop through London. Holmes contrived to look calm. I knew that he was counting the seconds, so I kept silent, and observed our metropole as it came to life.

There were few passengers leaving the city at this hour, and we quickly bought tickets and found an empty compartment. Almost at once, with a loud shriek from the whistle, the train set off. Without breakfast, I gratefully accepted Holmes' offered cigarette. Now I could relax, and I reminded him to tell me why we were here.

He replied brightly, pleased at my interest.

"Let me start at the beginning. Less than a half-hour before I woke you, Constable Gale was at our street door, trying to wake Mrs. Hudson and to persuade her that it was of the greatest urgency that she should bring him to me. When she did, I heard a rather vague account of a crime in the night in Sydenham. It seems an attempt was made to break into the Crystal Palace exhibition halls, but two watchmen had raised the alarm and given chase. The chase led into the park, where they lost sight of their quarry, but found a dead man.

"The police were informed, and the news went to Scotland Yard, since the local inspector had recently died and his post was still vacant. The consequence was that both Inspector

Lestrade and Inspector Gregson had been awoken and had hurried to the spot. Now, of all who might have been involved, these two are perhaps most properly to be considered the one-eyed among the blind. When they are together, they often seem to get in one another's way. Gregson had thought to send Constable Gale to call me. That is why we are here in the train to Sydenham, and we shall see what awaits us."

"Well, that certainly sounds mysterious, Holmes, and I wonder what it is that they are expecting you to investigate."

"Quite so, Watson, we shall see. They must need help, for they do not call me to all their murder cases! At least it has not rained, and it may be that we shall find on the ground some useful pointers to the events."

But then he spoke with some resignation, to say, "But of course, that will only be so if Gregson can prevent Lestrade and his men from disturbing everything."

As Holmes said this, he looked rather grimly about him, and there was silence in our compartment. I tried to change the subject. "Holmes, I must, to my shame, admit that I have never visited the Crystal Palace. Have you?"

"I recall that a trivial burglary in the Crystal Palace brought me here, many years ago, in the time when I did not have my faithful diarist at my side."

I might have asked what that might have been, but it interested him no more. He turned instead to a description, which lasted to our destination, of the many things that could be found in the Palace. I will not occupy you unnecessarily with all these details, but a short background may be helpful.

The Crystal Palace was first built in London's Hyde Park, for the Great Exhibition in 1851. Its name was perfect, for it was an engineering wonder, in glass and iron, in its dimensions and in its detail, which certainly justified its name as a palace. After the Exhibition it was in 1854 dismantled and rebuilt in Sydenham to be available to the public in perpetuity. A major exhibit was a collection of sculptures of peoples of all parts of the world, representing them from earliest times to the present. Holmes seemed to be impressed by the reconstructions of historic buildings, from old Egyptian times, from Greek works of art, the Colosseum in Rome and a most elaborate model of the Moorish Royal Palace, the Alhambra in Granada.

The extensive park adjoining the Crystal Palace is arranged in terraces of English and Italian tradition. There are also tennis courts, a cricket pitch, various athletics grounds, a boating lake and even an archery stand. As well as all this, there is a rich programme at all times of cultural activities and entertainments. A bearpit, a monkey house, and aviaries are there, and a challenging maze. Finally, I would mention the Geological Park, by the lake, which also has models of primitive creatures.

We arrived punctually at six forty-seven at our destination, and I was pleased to find there our tall fair-haired colleague, Inspector Gregson, waving his hat to greet us. He spoke briefly and assured Holmes that he had ensured as far as possible that nothing had been disturbed. We went together to the scene of the crime. From the Low Level station, we walked some 200 yards through a glazed gallery, to reach the southeast corner of the palace. We did not enter the palace, however, but passed through a side door into the gardens. Holmes and Gregson walked briskly on the neat gravel path, but I had some difficulty in keeping up with them, not only because of my irreparably injured leg with its Afghan war wound; I also found it all so impressive, that I stopped and turned several times to better admire this vast edifice. I learned later that the main hall of the palace is about 500 yards long, with various side aisles, two great side wings, and two transepts. There had been three transepts, but one was lost by a fire in 1866. The transepts are themselves over 100 yards long. The palace has two great water towers, which are some 300 ft high.

While I was attempting to take in all I saw of this size and beauty, I followed Holmes and Gregson as well as I could. The paths led through various flowerbeds, past statues, fountains and waterfalls. There were many places to rest, but I dared not stop, or I would lose sight of the two persons ahead of me. Ahead there appeared thick, and higher, privet hedges, which I could recognise as the maze, which Holmes had mentioned. Sure enough, as we came nearer, my suspicion became certainty, and this was clearly the place to which Inspector Gregson was bringing us. At the entrance to the maze, there were two persons of quite different stature waiting, the one a solid and burly police constable, guarding the entrance, and the other, very thin and nervous, who was walking restlessly up and down. Gregson introduced him as Mr. Irving, of the Crystal Palace administration.

My first impression proved to be correct. Mr. Irving appeared to be close to a breakdown and talked to us without pause. Although his remarks seemed to be confused and without any thread, one could see that his preoccupation was with the good reputation of the Crystal Palace, but Holmes and Gregson ignored him. They went straight into the maze, where I followed and Mr. Irving, still lamenting, fell in behind me. Gregson had a card in his hand, which was obviously a guide through the maze, because in a few minutes we reached the centre, a circular area with a wooden bench. It might otherwise have seemed attractive, but on this early morning of the 29th July there was no temptation to stay. A man's body lay on the wooden bench. His head had fallen back and revealed that his throat had been savagely and deeply cut. The wound had resulted in a heavy loss of blood. This had spread over his body as a repulsive red stain over his light summer suit. The gravel under the bench showed that there had been a large pool of blood, now however mostly soaked up in the soil beneath. This gruesome sight held my attention, so that Holmes' voice came to me as if from far away as he spoke to Inspector Gregson.

"Did you not tell me that the place had been kept undisturbed?"

"Indeed so, Mr. Holmes."

"But there seems to have been a herd of people tramping through the gravel and probably destroying any evidence."

"That, Mr. Holmes, was not to be avoided. First here were the watchmen from the Crystal Palace who found the body. One went to fetch the local constable who was on his beat in the neighbourhood. He had to see for himself, and then went to the police-station, from where the alarm was given. Scotland Yard was then told of the murder. From there I and Lestrade were called out and we made our own inspection of the scene."

I saw how Holmes' expression became more annoyed and irritated. He asked abruptly, "And what about the body?"

"The watchmen and the constable both assure me that they have not touched it. Neither have Lestrade and I."

If Inspector Gregson expected thanks from Holmes, he was disappointed. My friend drew his magnifying glass, fell on his knees, and started to study intently the bench and the body. I knew that this might be a lengthy process, and that I would be of no assistance to him. I came upon the idea that I might make up for our early start without breakfast. There might after all be an opportunity to find a cup of tea somewhere nearby. It might also help if I took Mr. Irving away with me for a short while, leaving Holmes free to concentrate. I turned to him and asked, "Mr. Irving, I know it is very early, but might we obtain something to eat and drink?"

My direct question confused him at first, but he then suddenly broke off his nervous litany of distress and answered, in a friendly tone, “Of course, Dr. Watson, please follow me.”

He then also drew a folded paper from his pocket, the key to the maze, and within a few minutes led me out at the entrance and then towards the main building. He insisted on accompanying me, and as I apologised with the hope that my request did not cause him trouble, he assured me that all was well.

“Please, Dr Watson, think nothing of it. The Crystal Palace is open in summer from 10 o’clock in the morning until 10 o’clock at night. From the third-class restaurant upwards, all sorts of refreshment may be found. We have public and private rooms, in addition to which there are numerous buffet counters.”

“You seem to have thought of every need, Mr. Irving.”

“Thank you, Dr. Watson, and indeed it is not only the catering which is important. Apart from the concerts and exhibitions, we also offer a library, a reading room, a laundry and washroom, a shoeshine, and a barber’s shop. But there is more, such as the possibility for the handicapped to hire for a few pence per hour a wheelchair with attendant, both in the palace and in the gardens.”

In view of the long walk, it was tempting to think of this; but had I expressed any need, I was sure that Mr. Irving would at once have set about meeting it, so I remained silent. We walked on silently a little further. I then asked him about the concerts.

"Yes, Dr. Watson, they are held all the year round. We can offer a wide variety, because we have all the resources here. Behind the entrance we are now approaching is the auditorium, the great stage, seating 4,000 guests. Here leading orchestras play daily.

"To the right of the great stage is the Opera House, seating 2,000. We play not only opera, but also drama and even our pantomimes. On the other side in our Handel Concert Hall, which seats 4,000 guests and is I am told, at more than 200 feet, twice the diameter of the dome of St Paul's in the City. The organ in the centre has 4,384 pipes and was built by Gray and Dawson. It is powered by a hydraulic pump. Our organist, E. J. Eyre, lectures almost daily on the character and functions of the organ. I can earnestly recommend that you come one day to hear him."

"Thank you, Mr. Irving. Although I must respect the work programme of Mr. Holmes, I would greatly appreciate such a visit."

He had indeed awakened my interest and curiosity.

We had reached the entrance and Mr. Irving insisted on taking me to the upper terrace, from where there was a dramatic view over the park and the county of Kent to the south.

Mr. Irving continued with the remark that the view from the North Tower was even better, because from there the eye could range over six counties and follow the River Thames to its mouth in the North Sea.

"Since however it is still very early, and remembering why you are here, I suggest that we satisfy our curiosity here, from this terrace, and that I now fetch your tea, and see whether there is already something to eat available in the kitchen."

First enquiries

I waited afterwards in the central transept for Holmes to enter. I was surprised to see him not only with Inspector Gregson, but also with another impressive looking gentleman, who was introduced as Mr. Arthur Higginson. It was obvious to me that Holmes was anxious to interview the two watchmen who had found the body. These were being questioned at present by Inspector Lestrade, who was using the Reading Room for that purpose. Holmes therefore went there, and we followed. I had therefore little opportunity to speak with Mr. Higginson, but I did learn that he was the murdered man's employer. The police had called him to identify the victim.

As we reached the Reading Room, Lestrade was concluding, and was ready to dismiss the two watchmen. On seeing the upright person of my friend, his face coloured, and he could not resist a somewhat sarcastic remark.

"Good morning, Mr. Holmes. What brings you to us? Could it just be that you have learned that a crime has been committed here?"

With his last words he threw a suspicious glance at Inspector Gregson. Holmes ignored the obvious implication, and said only, "Having carefully inspected the scene of the crime, my next task will be to interview the two watchmen who found the body."

Lestrade shrugged his shoulders and remarked, “Really, Mr. Holmes, if you have nothing better to do than look at trivia, then you are welcome to do so.”

Saying this, he beckoned Holmes into the Reading Room, and Mr. Higginson, somewhat embarrassed, asked Holmes if he would be needed again. Holmes assured him that he would indeed be needed, and for my part I had to comment on my surprise at Lestrade’s unpleasant manner.

“Inspector Lestrade, do I understand that for you, clearing up this murder is a trivial matter?”

“Indeed, Dr. Watson, the deceased in the park is clearly there as a consequence of the attempted break-in during the night. As soon as we have the person responsible, we will also have the murderer. And to do that it needs no cool intellectual deductions, and no exaggerated conclusions, but solid police work of the sort that we at Scotland Yard are accustomed to deliver.”

Lestrade spoke to me, but it was obvious that his remarks were directed at Holmes. Holmes however did not show any reaction, but simply continued as before. I therefore also refrained from further comment and showed no doubt about Lestrade’s words. Lestrade had in the meantime turned to Gregson. “Have you identified the victim?”

“Yes, Lestrade, He is Joseph Healy. His employer, Mr. Higginson, has identified him beyond doubt.” Gregson indicated Mr. Higginson, and asked, "Would you wish to speak with him?"

"I do not think that is necessary. We have now done all that we need to do, and the rest will now follow. I will now take the first train back to London. Gregson, would you wish to come with me?"

Inspector Gregson looked across to Holmes, who however avoided any show of interest. Gregson made up his mind, and with a firm voice said, "I will follow you later, and see you in the office."

"As you wish," said Lestrade. It was clear that Gregson did not agree with Lestrade that this was a trivial case. Nor, as I saw, did Holmes.

Holmes asked me if I would make notes, during the questioning of the watchmen, as I had often done in the past. I am thus able to bring you the subsequent conversations almost literally. Holmes asked each person separately. He began with Mr. William Cook, the older of the watchmen. He, when he was called, came with the typical bearing of an old soldier, summoned again on parade. Holmes had to ask him to take a seat before he would relax.

"Mr. Cook, please tell me what happened last night. Please omit nothing, even if it seems unimportant to you."

"Very good, Mr. Holmes." Holmes leaned back, closed his eyes, and brought his fingertips together. This may have seemed irritating, but I knew well that his concentration was never more sharply present than at such times. Mr. Cook showed no surprise and began at once with his account.

"Shortly after ten o'clock, after the last visitors had left the Palace and the Park, I began my usual rounds. As all gates were now locked, I left the Park and went to the Palace building, to make my normal round there. Nothing was unusual. I met then with Tom, that is with Thomas Jones, my colleague, and we exchanged a few words just there in the central transept. We heard a noise, which seemed to come from the park and gardens. As we came near to the glass doors, our lanterns must have surprised two young men, who were occupied with the doors. That is nothing new; attempted breaking in is not unusual, and our local police are seldom able to find those responsible. It will not surprise me if they can't catch last night's villains. Tom and I went after them, though. Now, my old legs are not as strong as they were, and I was soon out of breath. I couldn't keep up with Tom, and finally I had to sit on a bench and catch my breath again. I don't know how long it was, but suddenly there was Tom's voice calling me to come to the maze."

The watchman interrupted his account to mop his brow with a large handkerchief. It was clear that it was for him a burdensome exercise. In view of his age and his physique that was not altogether surprising. The doctor in me concluded that his days as a watchman were coming to an end. Many museums in London engaged old soldiers for such functions, and they were only too pleased to find an employment assuring them a place in civilian life.

Before I could reflect further, he began again.

“Tom had lost sight of the two lads in the vicinity of the maze and thought they might be hiding there. He wanted to go to see, although the maze was locked up. I wasn’t very eager, but you don’t leave a comrade on his own. We went in together, and then we found the murdered man in the centre, on a bench. My goodness, was that a shock, sir. It was not that I hadn’t seen enough dead ones in the past, but at that moment it was a complete surprise. When I looked more closely, I thought it was Joseph, that is, Joseph Healy, and I told the two inspectors that. You see, Joseph, and his brother, had both been employed here for some time as watchmen. His brother gave his notice a year ago, which was my good day as I obtained his position.

“I was always on good terms with Joseph, although we hardly ever saw one another apart from at work, because I live in Sydenham und he lived in Beckenham. I always said that he should live in Sydenham, where he was nearer to his work. I don’t know if he did anything about it, but one thing I can tell you, is that Joseph was always reliable and ready to help. And he always found time for a word in passing. That was so, even when he was no longer a watchman, but worked with Mr. Higginson, whom you have met. I told the inspectors from London that he works, no, worked, for this organiser of firework displays. I cannot imagine that he is dead, murdered, I rarely had such a generous and honest young man beside me. There is something behind this, and I hope you find it.”

Mr. Cook's voice rang suddenly hesitant, and he fished out his large handkerchief again to wipe his eyes. Then, as his feelings were calmer, there followed a little more.

"As Tom and I left the maze together, Tom went to find the local police constable, I waited on the bench near the ticket hut by the maze entrance. My legs are no longer so good…"

But we heard no more of this, for Holmes interrupted kindly and simply asked, "Thank you for your account, Mr. Cook. I have just one question for you."

"Yes, sir," he replied, mopping his forehead again.

Holmes asked, "Were you and Mr. Jones fearful of entering the maze?"

"No, sir, not at all, I know my way round with my eyes closed!"

"Indeed?" asked Holmes and made clear that it was for him of some importance.

"Certainly, sir, because every night before the wrought-iron gate is closed, it's our job to make a last round to see that no-one is locked in. When you do that every night you soon get to know the way round!"

"Thank you very much, Mr. Cook, that was very helpful," concluded Holmes. "Would you please now ask Mr. Jones to come in?"

Thomas Jones was a young man of about twenty-five years. Since he was, however, slim and not very tall, he seemed almost like a lad. He had red hair, and freckles in his otherwise pale face, and his uniform appeared a little too large for him. I thought I detected a hollow chest under his shirt and suspected that he had probably suffered rickets as a child, although the common spinal deformities that go with this were not apparent. But I came no further before Holmes started his questions.

"Mr. Jones, please tell me what happened last night, and leave nothing out, even if it seems of no importance." He took up again his familiar position, with eyes closed, fingertips together and leaning back. Jones, as have been many others, was at first puzzled, but then started to talk, in a somewhat piercing voice and appearing not to draw breath.

"I was on duty as usual, and so of course was Will, and as we met and made a short break in the central transept, we heard an unusual scratching noise. We looked, and there were two young men attempting to break in. Naturally we went after them. All at once they disappeared, and we thought they were hiding in the maze. We went to look, and what do we find? A corpse. I went straight away to find the local policeman, but when you want them they are never there. I finally found him, and he went first to the police station and came then to the maze. Then we all waited until the gentlemen from London arrived."

"Thank you, Mr. Jones," said Holmes, opening his eyes, "And now I have some questions for you. Were you and Mr. Cook always together while this was happening?" Mr. Jones hesitated, as if he had not understood the question, and then said, rather guardedly,

"Sir, you must understand that Will is rather older, and not in good health. He has a wife and three children and does his daily work well, but I know that Mr. Irving thinks Will should no longer work as watchman."

"Mr. Jones, please be reassured. My queries are in no way intended to have any personal consequences for you or Mr. Cook, unless of course you have done something improper."

"Oh no, sir, certainly not, there is nothing like that!"

Holmes then continued, "Then I may ask you again, Mr. Jones, were you together all the time after you noticed the attempted break-in?

"No sir, we were not. I followed the two suspects as far as the maze, and Will followed as best he could, until he was out of breath. That always happens when he has to move faster. I told him to sit down and wait by the maze, until I came with the policeman."

Holmes had followed carefully, and I was also forming a better opinion of Mr. Jones. He was not an impressive personality, and was perhaps not very bright, but apart from his strong sense of duty, which is naturally a watchman's strength, he had also shown me in these few minutes that he had a generous heart and nature, and that he would help his colleague as far as was in his power.

Holmes again continued, "Did you know the dead man?"

"I've often seen him in the park. Will told me he had worked here earlier."

"Now, Mr. Jones, can you tell me how I get to the centre of the maze?"

As he said this, he took a page from his notebook, and gave it, with his pencil, to the watchman. Jones was uncomfortable, and looked up and down, admitting, "I'm sorry, sir, I'm not much at writing."

"It will be enough if you simply indicate, in which direction I must turn at every opening. It is enough to write L or R for 'left' or 'right'." This calmed the watchman, so that he quickly annotated the paper. When he had finished, he gave it to Holmes who glanced at it and then placed it with his own papers, The interview ended, he now thanked Mr. Jones, dismissed him, and asked that Mr. Higginson would now enter the reading room.

When Mr. Higginson had taken his place, my friend began with his questions.

"Mr. Higginson, as I understand, you were asked by the police to come here to identify the murdered man?"

"Quite so, Mr. Holmes, and to my great regret I can only confirm, without doubt, that this was Joseph Healy."

"Would you know if there were anyone who might have had reason to do this? Had he differences with anyone?"

"I cannot imagine it, Mr. Holmes, as he was a most friendly person and even when he had, in the course of duty to be strict, he was always supported by his staff. I must tell you, that this has seriously disturbed me."

"He was, as I understand, an employee of yours."

"Yes, he was indeed my right hand, so to speak, and his death is for me, therefore, a particular shock."

Holmes asked, "What exactly did he do for you then, Mr. Higginson?"

"That will be clear if I tell you of what our work here consists of. I am one of the managers of the C.T. Brock Firework Company, and I am responsible for the firework displays every Thursday evening in summer, here at the Crystal Palace. It is always a most impressive display, and with good weather we often have 20,000 spectators. My principal concern is to ensure that the transport of materials, the construction of the display, and of course the performance, all take place exactly as we have planned. I have, of course, my specialist workers, who assure all the individual elements, but the overall planning and realisation is my responsibility. In doing this I am at my best, but I must admit that the working with others, the leading of teams and workpeople, was never something I really enjoyed. I think I am not a natural leader. In my job, of course, it has to be done, and here Joseph Healy, who had a natural gift, was my greatest asset."

He paused to reflect, sighed deeply, and then continued.

"Healy always saw to it that my instructions were followed and carried out. He would also lend a hand when it was needed, and no task was beneath his dignity. When he was hard at work, it was not difficult to realise that he was also very creative and, indeed, artistic. He had for example created a signboard and shield advertising in the best style the work and displays of our firm, C.T. Brock and Company. When he showed me this, I at once had a set of enamel panels made, which I had attached to the four large waggons which we use to transport our material. Perhaps three were enough, as all four waggons were never all in use, but who knows? Just in these days, we are heavily committed, as we have the honour of providing the huge firework display, which will be given tomorrow on the Thames, when the Prince of Wales will open the new Tower Bridge."

He sighed and then continued, "We receive, indeed, requests from people who for whatever reasons would like to have one of our advertising panels. Last week, disgraceful to relate, we even had one stolen, and will have to think of replacing it. Mind you, as a businessman I have always to reckon with a certain wastage. We are in the public eye, and one must always reckon with human weakness. I find this to be an attitude which makes our way through life a little easier. Healy however could not accept this. For him, everything had to be correct and accurate. That is indeed why I also entrusted to him our bookkeeping and accounts. He was most precise, and a penny too much or too little was unknown. When I once praised him, he admitted that sometimes he had repeatedly gone through the accounts, to find errors of which he had become aware. He disliked discrepancies, as indeed earlier this week, when he determined that six large wooden crates, in which we customarily transport fireworks, were missing. I was naturally very concerned, as six large crates of fireworks represent a substantial value for our company. Healy went through our inventory and told me that the crates were missing after a delivery, and that they must therefore have been empty. I assured him then that C.T. Brock and Co. would scarcely miss six empty wooden crates. Even so, I had the feeling that he was still checking the delivery and stock lists, to find out where they might be."

Higginson ended his rather lengthy account, and for a moment all was still. Holmes however had a further question.

"Thank you, Mr. Higginson. Tell me, please, how did you become aware that Mr. Healy might be a suitable employee with you?"

"Of course, Mr. Holmes. I had placed an announcement in several newspapers. He was one who replied, among various suitable candidates, and he gave the best overall impression. It was certainly good that, as he worked at the Crystal Palace, he was familiar with it."

"And was it part of his job to be here last night, as the firework display was presented?"

"No, not directly; he was not involved in the display itself, or in setting off any fireworks. He was often here, however, just to be reassured, and to inform me that all was as we wished it to be."

"He would perhaps have had to visit the park outside the usual opening hours?"

"Quite right, Mr. Holmes; for that purpose he had, as did the watchmen, a fully authorised set of keys."

"Thank you, Mr. Higginson, for your most interesting information. You may now go home, but I would be grateful if you could give me Mr. Healy's lodging address."

"That I can do at once," he replied and reached into his jacket to produce a black notebook. He thumbed through and muttered, as if by explanation, that when the police constable had called in the early morning to tell him of the murder, and suggesting it might be one of his employees who would have to be identified, he had at once brought the notebook with him, as it contained details for all his staff. He glanced somewhat critically at Inspector Gregson, and added, "But so far none of the police has asked me for it."

He looked back to Holmes, smiled and said, "I am pleased that I thought to bring it. So can I be of real assistance in this most regrettable affair. The address is: Mrs. Amelia Bolger, 5 Queens Road, South Norwood."

After I had noted the address, and Mr. Higginson had taken his leave, Holmes turned to me. "Have you been able to record all the information, Watson?"

"Yes, I am sure, Holmes," I replied, although I was not so certain that I could say what was really important, or not.

But Holmes had turned to Inspector Gregson. "What did you think, of what we have heard?"

Gregson took his time, and then replied, "Well, it was certainly all very… interesting. We have now a much better picture of the events and of the victim. I do not see, however, at this point, how it will help us to clear up the murder. Perhaps Lestrade was right after all…"

But he came no further, as at this moment a knock on the door announced a messenger with a telegram for him.

He read it quickly and said without further emotion, "I regret that I will have to take my leave of you at once." Without explanation he showed us the telegram. It read

Gregson - Body in Thames, London Docks district. Await you at Scotland Yard - Lestrade

He was already turning to leave, but looked over his shoulder and said, "Please keep me informed." Then he raised his hand and left.

We sat for a few moments in silence. Alone in the Reading Room, I was now uneasy, even helpless. Breaking the silence, I said, "And what shall we do next, Holmes?" It was as if I had woken him from a deep sleep.

His eyes lit up, and he jumped to his feet. "We will visit the lodging of the murdered man!" he exclaimed suddenly, and walked out, bidding me to follow him.

The next steps

We left the Crystal Palace as the doors were being opened for the public. The corpse had been removed, and nothing was now there to signal that a brutal and gruesome crime had been committed during the night. Holmes guided me through the various passages and galleries, and surprised me with his obviously extensive knowledge. We emerged at the Low Level station. Here we had arrived, earlier that morning, from London Bridge, but now we were to take the train in the opposite direction, It would only be a short journey of some five minutes, for we alighted at Norwood Junction, where the train stopped. A cab soon drew up at the station entrance, and so we took it to continue our journey, through Albert Road and then into the almost circular terrace formed by Lincoln Road and Queens Road. Here trees bordered the road, and most houses were individual two-storey homes, each with a small front garden. We were soon at our destination and Holmes asked the driver to wait. That he did gladly, for Holmes assured him a gratuity for his patience. I noticed that there was a small notice on the fence, announcing "Room to let."

Soon at the front door, we rang the bell. There was a pause, and the door was opened. An older lady stood before us and regarded us questioningly. We greeted her, raising our hats.

"Good morning, gentlemen," she replied.

Holmes asked politely, "Would you be Mrs. Bolger, the landlady in this house?"

"Yes, sir, I am indeed. Please forgive me that you had to wait; I was in the back garden."

Holmes began at once to introduce us. "My name is Sherlock Holmes, and this is my colleague Dr. Watson."

Mrs. Bolger looked troubled, and she answered with some concern, "Oh dear, sirs, I fear I must disappoint you. I only have a single room now to let, and although it has a good view and is well-furnished, it is in truth only suitable for a single person."

She reminded me of our good and thoughtful Mrs. Hudson in Baker Street, and so I spoke, before Holmes could reply, to say, "Please do not be concerned about that, Mrs. Bolger. We have not come to ask about the room."

That was at once a relief and a source of irritation for Mrs. Bolger. "But why then would you be ringing at my door?"

It was now a very delicate moment, to explain the true reason for our call, and although I knew Holmes was always very courteous and respectful to ladies, I could only hope that he could find the right words. I did not envy him his task at this moment.

"Mrs. Bolger," he said gently, "I deeply regret to have to tell you that your tenant, Mr. Healy, was this morning in the early hours found dead."

As Holmes said this, all colour drained from her face. She looked at him with incredulity and then stammered, "Dead? But he was such a young man. Has he had an accident?"

"No, Mrs. Bolger, he was the victim of a criminal act."

I saw how Mrs. Bolger swallowed suddenly, how the shock showed in her eyes, and how her hand sought a hold on the doorhandle. While I looked to see if my services might be needed, Holmes continued with his explanation, although it was not quite the whole truth.

"The police are already investigating the crime, and as I have often helped Scotland Yard with their enquiries, they have asked me to do so again. For that I have come to speak with you, Mrs. Bolger. It is most important that I and my colleague Dr. Watson see the room in which Mr. Healy was staying with you."

Mrs. Bolger followed these explanations with care and replied, "Of course, Mr. Holmes, I would naturally wish to help the police, please come in and follow me."

Obviously unsteady, but now a little recovered from her first shock, she led us through the house, up the narrow staircase to the upper floor. She opened the door to Mr, Healy's room, and we all entered. The room was most orderly and made a good and fresh impression. My eyes wandered over the furnishings, a cupboard and a chest of drawers, a table with two chairs, and a couch with a small coffee table. A curtain fell across the room where it concealed the section where was the bed, a bedside table, and another chest of drawers with a marble top. Standing on this were the usual bowl and water jug for washing and shaving. Holmes was soon occupied in a detailed examination, with his magnifying glass, of the room and its contents, so I sat with Mrs. Bolger at the table to talk with her.

.

Once seated, I took out my notebook and began with questions such as I had so often heard Holmes ask in his work. "Mrs. Bolger, how long has Mr. Healy been your tenant?"

"I can't say to the day," she replied, "but it must be around a year. He had as I recall lived earlier in Beckenham."

"Do you know if he had any differences or disagreements with anybody?"

"I really cannot imagine it, Dr. Watson, because Joseph is, sorry, was, such a quiet and helpful tenant. He had often helped me on the weekends in the garden, and he always paid the rent regularly, on the first of the month. He was very correct, also in other aspects of his life. He always left the house at the same time, and I could have set the clock by that. It was indeed curious to me that this morning the jug of hot water, which I had brought, as every morning, had not been touched. I thought he had perhaps come home late the previous evening and had slept on. I would never have imagined that Joseph …"

Here she broke off, and the tears now welling up were too much for her. She pulled a handkerchief from her apron pocket and wept quietly into it. I offered some words of comfort, and saw then that Holmes was on hands and knees, studying every detail. Mrs. Bolger came slowly back to herself, calm but quiet, and as I saw that she interested herself in Holmes' examination, I decided to ask her more.

"Mrs. Bolger, can you tell me anything of Mr. Healy's family? Or do you know whether he perhaps had one or two close friends?"

"Dr. Watson, as I said before, he was a most helpful and friendly person, and I am sure he had friends. Who or where they were is quite unknown to me. Concerning his family, I think he has mentioned a brother, or perhaps a cousin. I think he once told me that his parents both died when he was very young, but even that is not certain. You know, surely, that with increasing age, memory can play tricks on us."

That this was so, I had observed many times, and not always only in my practice. But before we could talk further, Holmes stood up and came to our table. He had a framed photograph in his hands and addressed himself to Mrs. Bolger.

"Do you know this young lady?"

"I'm sorry, Mr. Holmes, but I do not."

What Holmes' thoughts were at this, I could not ascertain, He put the photograph on the table, and continued, "I have also found a second photograph. Perhaps you can help me with this one. Would you please look at it?"

He went to the chest of drawers, and opened the top drawer, to withdraw from it a long photograph, also framed. We all looked at it carefully, Mrs. Bolger doing so with the aid of Holmes' magnifying glass. The photograph showed a number of persons, and without the glass it was difficult to see details. I could however identify a man in the centre, dressed in a business suit, seated on a chair. Beside him was a woman, and the two were flanked by two men in their shirtsleeves. In the foreground was a lad, who was holding up a notice.

"Well, now," said Mrs. Bolger, "the faces are small, and not clear in my eyes, but I am sure that the right-hand man in shirtsleeves is poor Joseph. Who the others are I do not know."

Holmes nodded gratefully to these words, and then, as if quite out of context, asked, "Would you know Hooper's shop, for groceries and provisions?"

"No, Mr. Holmes, I never heard of it, but it is surely not here in Norwood. You will understand that I know Norwood intimately, as I have lived here all my life."

Holmes risked a satisfied smile, but it disappeared at once as he continued. "To continue my work, I fear I will have to take these two photographs with me."

"Well, Mr. Holmes, as you are helping the police, I am sure that is all right. But what if…"

Holmes took up the question she was hesitating to ask. “What, if a relative of Mr. Healy wishes to have them?”

She nodded in agreement.

“Should that happen, you must send them to me, saying that the photographs may be collected at this address.” With these words, he took his visiting cards, and laid one on the table. “Thank you, Mr. Holmes,” replied Mrs. Bolger, visibly relieved, and Holmes took the two photographs and carefully put them into a large inside pocket of his jacket.

“I must thank you, Mrs. Bolger”, said Holmes, “But now we must continue on our way.”

With these words he turned abruptly, left the room, and hurried down the stairs. Mrs. Bolger was somewhat surprised and looked to me for reassurance. I however also did not know what was occupying him at this moment, and I could only shrug my shoulders and thank her politely, before hurrying after Holmes.

I had done my best to hurry and follow him, but even so, Holmes was already in the cab and waiting for me. The moment I was seated, beside him, our cabman cracked his whip and we left in haste. Holmes obviously wanted to remain silent during the journey, for he showed no reaction to my remark about the visit to Mrs. Bolger. As I sat silently, I was thus all the more surprised when he said, obviously in a good humour, “We are in luck, Watson. Our cabman knows the district around Holy Trinity Church in Sydenham very well, as he often brings passengers to the Crystal Palace Cemetery."

This meant nothing to me. I asked him, "Holy Trinity Church in Sydenham?" He nodded as an answer, which left me no wiser. "Perhaps you will tell me why we are going to this church?"

He looked at me, first irritated and then sympathetically. "Watson, you did not hear correctly. I did not say that we were going to the church, but that our cabman knows this quarter well. That is important, because he knows Hooper's grocery and provisions shop which is there in Croydon Road."

It now became clear. It was however not apparent to me, why we should be visiting this shop. I told him this, and as answer, he took the longer framed photograph from his pocket, and gave me his magnifying glass to look at it again.

"Look at the door of the shop, Watson, and you will see what is engraved on the glass. Can you read it, old friend?" Adjusting my angle in the bad light, I suddenly saw what he meant.

Groceries and Provisions, Proprietor Paul Hooper.

"Well done, Watson. This photograph was taken to mark the twenty-fifth anniversary of the founding of this business. That is what the notice tells us, which the lad in the foreground is holding up."

I looked again with the glass and saw "25 Years" carefully written on the notice. Before I could comment, he continued.

"Photographs which are taken on such occasions are always arranged in the same way, whether it is a small business or indeed a factory. In the background are all or part of the premises, in the middle is the proprietor, and respectfully arranged around him are the staff. The rule is, that the nearer they are to the owner, the more significant they are in the business. Should there be children, they are placed, sitting or kneeling, in front."

I followed with great interest, and said, "Then the older gentleman on the chair is the proprietor, Mr. Paul Hooper."

"Quite so, Watson. And who is the young lady beside him? That is most probably a daughter, because she is standing at his side, and her right hand is on his shoulder. Apart from that, both have the same high forehead, the same striking cheekbones, and a curiously narrow nose."

I looked again at the photograph through the glass, and could confirm what Holmes had said. I nodded my agreement and concluded, "As the landlady has confirmed that the young man in shirtsleeves is the murdered Mr. Healy, we may conclude that he had worked for a while in Mr. Hooper's store, and as you obviously want to find out more about Mr. Healy, which is why you visited Mrs. Bolger, we are now going to visit Hooper's Grocery and Provisions shop."

"Correct, Watson, you have thought that out quite logically."

That pleased me, for Holmes was always most economical with his praise. I smiled, and he continued, "But there is a further reason why I must visit Mr. Hooper as soon as possible."

I looked questioningly at Holmes, who by way of answer drew out the portrait photograph of the young woman, which he had also found in Mr. Healy's room at Mrs. Bolger's house. He showed it to me with the remark that he was certain the portrait showed the same person as did the group photograph.

Holmes' magnifying glass again served to confirm to me that he was almost certainly correct in his assumption. I said as much, but he had now already slipped into one of those introspective moments where he took no more notice of other ideas. We therefore sat silently together until I had to ask the question occupying me for some time.

"Holmes, I share your view that we must visit Mr. Hooper and his daughter as quickly as possible, especially since he appears to hold her in some affection. She must not learn of his death from a newspaper report. But how did you know that the business was in Sydenham?"

"It was a hypothesis which I set out to test, by logical thinking, and I was fortunately able with the help of our cabdriver to confirm it at once. You will recall that Healy worked in Sydenham, as a watchman at the Crystal Palace, and later with the fireworks company of C.T. Brock and Co. He had latterly lived in Norwood, and prior to that in Beckenham. His life was largely therefore concentrated upon Sydenham. It seemed therefore well possible that the woman for whom he had, as you so carefully expressed it, some affection, should also live somewhere in this district. Apart from that, I found in one of the drawers in Mr. Healy's room a Bible which was of unusual interest."

"Confirming his faith?"

"That surely Watson, but what was printed on the first page was a notice, that this was a special print, not on sale to the public. This Bible was printed specially by order of the Church of Holy Trinity in Sydenham. This discovery, and the consideration that Beckenham was really too far out of the way to have supported a business such as Mr. Hooper's for twenty-five years, including its assortment of exotic colonial produce, then with the categoric statement of Mrs. Bolger that there was no such store in Norwood, increased for me the probability that it was in Sydenham. I asked the cab driver and he confirmed on the spot my suspicion. Had we not had a cab driver with this knowledge, I would surely have found it out, but we would have spent more time and energy getting there. You have however already remarked that it is a matter of urgency that we get to Hooper's as quickly as possible. I fear something serious is afoot."

I could ask no more as we were already at our destination in Croydon Road.

A depressing visit

Holmes once again instructed the cab driver to wait. I, in the meantime, studied the front of the building. At the centre was the door with the engraving revealed to me by the magnifying glass. On either side of the door there were shop windows.

As we entered the shop by the door, a bell rang clearly, announcing us as customers. An older man emerged from the back of the store, and I was almost certain that it was the man on the photograph who was seated in the centre on a chair. This time he was not in a business suit, but was now in his shirtsleeves, and wore a long apron. It seemed that he had difficulty in walking, for he let one leg hang back, while he attempted to take the weight of the other by supporting himself with his hands, on his various stands and boxes. Nevertheless, he greeted us with a friendly smile.

"A good day to you, gentlemen, how can I help you?"

"Are you Mr. Paul Hooper, the proprietor of this business?" asked Holmes.

"I am indeed," said Mr. Hooper cheerfully

"My name is Sherlock Holmes, and this is my colleague, Dr. Watson".

"Glad to meet you, gentlemen," Hooper again replied cheerfully.

There was a short pause, and Mr. Hooper looked at us questioningly. I must, to my shame, admit that it was Holmes' task, and not mine, to bring bad news.

"Mr. Hooper, do you know Joseph Healy?"

"Of course I do, Mr. Holmes, last Saturday he and my daughter Annie celebrated their engagement."

As he said this, I had suddenly to think of my dear Mary, whom I had now lost for ever. This thought went directly to my heart, and my expression must have shown my anxiety, for Mr. Hooper turned to me and asked earnestly, "Has something happened to Joseph? Is he in trouble? Has there been an accident? … What have you come to tell me?" I could not speak, and Holmes answered for me.

"We have the unpleasant task of informing you and your daughter of the death of Mr. Joseph Healy. He was the victim of a violent crime and Scotland Yard has already begun an investigation. Since Dr. Watson and I have often assisted Scotland Yard, they have asked us to assist in their investigation. I fear that we have to ask you and your daughter some questions."

Mr. Hooper had followed my friend's words with an expression of unbelief. All colour had left his face, and he sat down unsteadily on a crate to stare forward with empty eyes. He sat silently, and finally spoke.

"How dreadful… why, oh God, why… oh, Annie, my poor, poor Annie…."

He drew out a handkerchief, and wiped his eyes. When he was sure he could again speak clearly, he called "Jack," in a sharp voice. A youth appeared at once, apparently the one in the photograph who was holding the jubilee notice. He stood in front of Mr. Hooper, who said quietly, "I must take these two gentlemen upstairs. Please remain in the shop until I come down again."

"Yes, Mr. Hooper," the youth replied, and looked at us with unveiled curiosity, as we followed Mr Hooper upstairs.

He showed us into a small salon, and left us then, so as to talk privately with his daughter and inform her himself of Joseph's death. He had promised to bring her then to speak with us, as far as she was, after this tragic news, able to do so.

Some time passed, and then the door opened, and Annie Hooper entered, with her father behind her. Despite her tear-stained face and red eyes, it was apparent that she had a naturally gentle and quite pretty face. We had on her entry stood, of course, and as Mr. Hooper introduced us, we both expressed our sympathy. She nodded in acknowledgment. Once we were seated at the round table in the centre of the room, there was a moment of silence. I heard the ticking of the grandfather clock, seemingly intrusively loud. I took out my note book and hoped that Holmes would find all the tact and calm necessary for such a conversation. He turned to her and spoke very gently.

"Miss Hooper, I must sincerely thank you that you have agreed to speak with us. It is for our purpose extraordinarily important to learn as much as possible about Mr. Joseph Healy, because it may help us to find out what led to his murder and who is responsible."

Miss Hooper nodded as Holmes spoke, and the first question followed. "Miss Hooper, how long have you known Mr. Healy?"

Her voice was at first unsteady and hoarse, but she cleared her throat and at the next attempt her words were not only clear and easy to understand, but her voice was even warm and agreeable on the ear.

"I met Joseph during last autumn, at the Harvest Festival fair at Holy Trinity Church in Sydenham. Among the various entertainments on offer, there was also a sale of tickets with a draw for prize winners. There were generous prizes, including a basket of fruit given by my father. Another was of two bottles of port wine, from the wine shop in the Anerley Road, and as first prize a handsome embossed leatherbound Bible, given by the vicar, the Reverend Pearce. The lottery was in aid of our fund for distressed members of the parish. I was engaged to sell tickets, and so became aware of a young man, who appeared, during the course of the afternoon, to have bought a considerable number of my tickets. This young man was Joseph. We chatted agreeably, and laughed together, especially as he suggested, in strict confidence, of course, that he might win the two bottles of port, with me to bring him good fortune. He did indeed win the draw, but won the first prize, the Bible."

Here she paused briefly. A weak smile passed over, and her eyes lit up, but it passed quickly, and her face was again empty of expression.

"From then on, Joseph attended Holy Trinity Church regularly, every week, with me and with my father. After the service there are always tea and pastries in the vicarage of Reverend Pierce, and so we found occasion to talk more frequently, and an affection between us grew from these regular meetings."

Since Miss Hooper was again silent, her father spoke up. "I had obviously observed this," he said "and decided to learn more about Joseph. I invited him after church to visit the house, and I was most agreeably impressed by his behaviour, and also his quiet manner. I enjoyed talking with him. He did not much talk of himself, but seemed to be well informed, with wide interests, and certainly not full of his own opinions. Moreover, Joseph was always energetic and helpful. That this was so became very evident, as, shortly before Christmas, I had a severe fall, the consequence of which was that for some weeks I could hardly leave my bed.

"As Joseph heard of this, he gave up his job at the Crystal Palace, in order to support Annie, for it would have been impossible for a woman alone to manage such a grocery business. Naturally it was not at once easy, because there was a lot to learn, especially in the accounts and bookkeeping. But

I can assure you, Mr. Holmes, that I would not like to think what would have become of us, had Joseph not been there to help us."

He wiped his eyes and his nose again, before saying, "From that time on I knew that in Joseph I would have a son-in-law who would take the business, which has been my life's work, into the future, making Annie happy and ensuring that she would want for nothing."

With these words, Mr. Hooper looked affectionately to his daughter, and laid his hand gently on hers, which appeared to be held together in prayer. A silence fell again in the small room. Each had his or her own thoughts. My own loss came again painfully to mind, and as I felt my throat tightening and the tears close, I occupied myself with my notebook. I perhaps would thus not look as helpless as I felt. I was relieved, that Holmes came with another question.

"Miss Hooper, did you see Mr. Healy yesterday?"

"Yes, Mr. Holmes, in the late afternoon, but only briefly, for half an hour. I had some purchases to make, and almost bumped into him as he was entering the telegraph office, obviously deep in thought. He accompanied me on the way home and took his leave to go directly to the Park of the Crystal Palace, where he had to attend the last preparations for last night's firework display."

She took a breath before continuing.

"You need to know, Mr. Holmes, that Joseph was, in the last two weeks, very busy. Apart from the weekly display in the Crystal Palace, he was also responsible for the planning and installation of the fireworks which will follow the inauguration by the Prince of Wales, of the new Tower Bridge in London. This week most of his time was spent between the new bridge, and a nearby warehouse in the London docks where the materials for the display have been stored. Whenever he was back in Sydenham, he helped my father, who is now thankfully a little recovered, and he was on Thursday able to give attention to the display at the Crystal Palace."

She paused again. "I would have been much happier if Joseph could have worked all the time in the shop until our wedding, but he did not wish to do that. He explained that it would not be right, if he, practically without resources, should marry the future owner of a flourishing business. His opportunity to earn some money of his own was the firework business, and he saved every penny from that. He paid his rent from the wages my father paid him. He did it all to ensure that he would not stand before the altar with empty pockets."

Miss Hooper fought again with her tears, and I felt spontaneous sympathy for her situation. Holmes saw that another question was now needed.

"Miss Hooper, did Mr. Healy have any enemies?"

"No, Mr. Holmes. He has – he had such an agreeable personality, and was quite naturally with the people around him always on the best of terms…"

"Except for Reuben," said her father suddenly. We looked at him for an explanation.

"Reuben is Joseph's younger brother. After my fall, Joseph brought him from time to time to help in the shop, and he is certainly as strong as an ox. He could take up the work of two mature men, and that, although he had lost the thumb of his right hand. The problem is that he cannot handle any job without supervision. Joseph or I always had to tell him everything wanted doing and stand over him while he did it. Not only that, but he was quite without moral scruples. He did not hesitate to help himself and take things out of the shop, and we only found out as we were making up the books. He really should not have done that, as I paid him for his work, even though it was only casual work. He also had a regular job at the gasworks in Lower Sydenham."

While Mr. Hooper gave us this information, Holmes had spread out the long photograph, which he had kept in his pocket. He then said, "Mr. Hooper, this photograph was among Mr. Healy's affairs. He is here on the right-hand side. Can I take it that the young man on the other side is Reuben Healy?"

"Yes, Mr. Holmes, we had the picture taken in March at the 25th anniversary of our business here. Joseph and Reuben had to carry me then, from upstairs, so that I could take my place before the shop, because my own legs would not carry me. I must admit that that was very difficult, and painful, and that it was a great relief to be back on my bed."

Holmes nodded, and then continued, "You said that the two brothers had their differences, Mr. Hooper."

"Quite so, Mr. Holmes. I knew from Joseph that they had argued and had their differences, concerning the work itself, and also because of Reuben's stealing goods and objects. But the worst came in early April, as they came to blows on the street."

Mr. Hooper looked across at his daughter Annie.

She said, with some embarrassment,

"Yes, I was the reason. Reuben, during the time he was in the shop, became more and more offensive, and despite my repeated rejection of his advances, he kept trying to approach me. Joseph, as he became aware, spoke sharply to Reuben and the affair ended, as my father told me, in a most unseemly brawl on the street outside. I did not see Reuben again after that. Joseph, however, had a letter from him, some four weeks ago, saying that he had found another job in the Millwall Docks and had taken a room nearby in the public house known as The Ship's Wheel in Market Street. He also asked Joseph to help him because he had lost a lot of money at cards and could not pay the rent. Joseph determined to go to The Ship's Wheel, meet the landlord, Mr. Samuel Knox, and pay the money personally to him. He did indeed see his brother but refused to give him money directly. He clearly thought that Reuben would only lose it again or drink himself into a stupor. That had already happened when they were both watchmen at the Crystal Palace. Joseph had tried to keep it quiet and do the work of both of them but had finally given Reuben the choice: either no more alcohol or leave. If not, he would have to tell the administration."

Another pause for breath.

"It hurt Joseph to have to threaten his brother in this way, and not to yield to his begging. This needs explanation. The parents had both died very young, and Joseph had always taken responsibility for his brother, as they were passed from one relative to another, nobody really wanting more mouths to feed. The last of these was a fisherman in Plymouth, and there the two brothers, in the hope of a better life, ran away, and signed on to go to sea. I don't know how long they were away, but Reuben once tried to impress me with the tattoos on his arm, which were he said, a souvenir for each port of call. It shocked me as there were so many, and I can only assume he was away quite a long time."

Miss Hooper stopped again, and her breathing became rapid and shallow. The long description had obviously been a strain in her present acute distress.

"And there were no more letters between them?" asked Holmes.

"Joseph had told me of nothing more," she replied. "But Reuben did not even reply to the invitation to our engagement…"

At this thought, her self-control, at which I had frankly wondered, broke down and she began to sob helplessly, the tears streaming down. Her face was a heart-breaking picture of the pain she felt, and she suddenly stood up and left the room.

We stood as she left and remained standing in silence, looking at the open door, through which she had disappeared. Suddenly I heard the quiet voice of Holmes.

"Mr. Hooper, I thank you most sincerely for your invaluable help. I have at present nothing more, but should there be any further need, I will ask you."

Mr. Hooper understood, nodded, and then said thoughtfully, "I think it is best now if my Annie first has the time to weep over her Joseph. Come, gentlemen, I will show you to the door."

Questions and Answers

Our cabman brought us back to the Low Level station at the Crystal Palace, and we took the first train back to London Bridge. After visiting Hooper's shop, we both fell into a deep silence. Each of us had his own thoughts on what we had seen and heard. The trains at this time were not busy, and we found an empty first-class compartment, to sit as we had so often, facing one another.

As the train started. I asked Holmes if I might open the window. He muttered what I took as agreement, but it was clear that he was now deep in thought. I lifted the leather strap off its rest and allowed the window to fall a few inches, before making the strap secure again. The recent days had been very hot, and the stream of air was more than welcome. Leaning back comfortably, I saw Holmes, also leaning back, his eyes closed, and his hands stretched out, the fingertips touching. He was deep in thought. In order not to disturb him I watched the scene passing before the window, as we approached London Bridge station. I found myself asking if we were really any wiser about the case before us, which might help in explaining the murder of Joseph Healy. I decided, before we arrived, to break the silence and ask.
"Holmes, what do you plan to do next?"

My friend opened his eyes slowly, as if from a deep sleep, looked at me and said, "We are going to visit Mr. Reuben Healy."

"Will you then tell him of his brother's death, and also ask him your questions?" Holmes smiled nervously and looked at me mildly amused.

"I suspect, Watson," he said, "that Reuben Healy is all too well aware of the circumstances of his brother's death." I needed a moment to realise what he meant.

"But Holmes, does that mean that you believe that Reuben has murdered his own brother?" I replied sharply, with the further remark that a rejected affection for the shopkeeper's daughter, weeks before, could hardly justify such an act. I was undoubtedly agitated, because, for me, a murder between brothers was practically unthinkable; but Holmes was a picture of calm, when he addressed me with a sorrowing smile and with a soberly practical answer.

"Calm yourself, my friend. For you such a crime is inconceivable, but the history books tell us that there is here nothing unusual. And that is quite apart from the Bible with its story of Cain and Abel but let us concentrate on Mr. Reuben Healy. It was not his rejection by Miss Hooper, but rather the place and manner of the crime, which lead me to my conclusion."

Holmes had seen my confusion and offered his explanation.

"As I examined the victim in the park, I saw that his throat had been practically severed. This was not the wound of a small, sharp blade, such as the scalpel of a doctor, but rather the kind of wound made by a knife such as fishermen and seamen carry. To make such a cut with a seaman's knife requires however great strength. I also noted that in order to do the deed, the murderer stood behind his victim, and, with a free hand, held the victim's mouth closed and pulled his head back. All this requires an unusually strong man determined to do his worst."

"I next observed in my examination that the fatal wound was, from the victim's view, delivered from right to left. That indicated clearly that it was administered by a left-handed person. It was also interesting to see that there was no sign that a struggle or fight had taken place. The knife attack must have been a complete surprise, and this suggests that the victim was not aware of any danger, and that the murderer must therefore have been a person already known to him. A stranger might have aroused a natural suspicion.

"Now let us consider what Mr. and Miss Hooper told us about Reuben:

- He is an unusually strong young man. He has therefore the strength, something I consider necessary for the crime.
- As a boy he was for some time, with his brother, looked after by a relative who was a fisherman, and then went to sea. It is no surprise, if he then possesses a seaman's knife, such as was used for the crime.
- During childhood he lost his right thumb. He would naturally use his left hand, then, whenever he had to hold something

securely. As a doctor, Watson, you will surely confirm that to use such a knife needs a safe, firm grip."

Holmes broke off his thoughts here to draw a cigarette from his silver case. He offered me one, and I took it gratefully in the hope it would help to calm my nerves. I had followed Holmes' account but was still not really convinced that Reuben could be the murderer. After all, except for the matter of knowing one another, everything that he had said could also apply to many other persons.

There was however more to come.

"Now let us consider the crime.

"The centre of the maze is surely a most remarkable place for a crime. It is however an ideal place to organise an undisturbed meeting. I suspect that Joseph Healy had, in fact, invited his brother to meet him there. What the reason was, we do not yet know, and all else is speculation. Perhaps it had to do with the engagement party. Perhaps his brother had again been asking for money, and he wanted to teach him a lesson before giving him more, Whatever the reason, they met in the park at the maze, which, given the professional commitments of Joseph, and his limited time, was surely easiest for him. The two brothers needed a private place for a personal conversation. They went to the maze. Joseph knew the way through it, and, as his employer Mr. Higginson had confirmed, he had a set of keys to go anywhere in the park. The two brothers met, talked until the conversation escalated out of hand, and the murder followed. And now comes a most important question."

I interrupted Holmes to say, "But of course, the time! Am I right, Holmes?" His disapproval showed his annoyance, that I had interrupted him.

"Watson, the time of the murder is important, partly because it shows that Lestrade's suspicion is absurd. That was not, however, what I was going to say yet."

He saw my uncomprehending expression, and suddenly said, "All right, Watson, let us look first at the time. The watchman, William Cook, told us that the maze was always closed at sunset. It is before this time regularly checked. That means that murderer and victim could only have come later upon the scene. We also know from Mr. Cook that the blood was dried when he found the body. That, given the quantity from a slit throat, would have taken some time. This suggests that the murder must have taken place during the firework display."

I nodded. "That seems clear, Holmes, but what was now the second question?"

"How did the murderer get out of the maze? As I examined the pockets of the victim, I noticed that his keys to the park were missing. It seems that the murderer took the keys in order to get out. But the keys alone are of little help when one is lost in a maze. Whether or not they had a lantern was of no assistance. The question in my mind from the start of my investigation was, how did the murderer get out of the maze?

We asked both watchmen this morning, and received from each, in their own way, the answer – that every watchman knows the paths through the maze. Knowing this left me sure that a former watchman could very well be the culprit. Watchman Cook however also confirmed this morning that the brother of Joseph had for a time worked as a watchman. That had to form part of my suspicion of Reuben."

I had followed with interest, but it did then occur to me that there might have been another explanation. I asked him directly. "Holmes, as we came upon Inspector Gregson this morning, he used a plan of the maze to lead us. Mr. Irving also used such a plan, as he took me out to satisfy my wish for a cup of tea. Could it not be that the murderer also had such a plan?"

He smiled and said, "The question is certainly justified, Watson. It could not be excluded, but I ascertained from Inspector Gregson that there are only two examples of this plan, both mounted on a card, in existence. The one, which Gregson had, is normally in the restroom of the watchmen. The other, which Mr. Irving had, is kept in the ticket office at the entrance to the maze, for emergencies."

At least Holmes had not dismissed my question as irrelevant, and so I voiced another thought. "Holmes, had you considered that after the crime, the murderer might not have left the maze on the gravel path, but by breaking through one of the hedges?"

"Indeed, as I started my investigation, I explored this possibility. I soon rejected it, however, because, despite not having the opportunity to examine all the hedges, I saw at once that they are very thick and strong. It is not possible to break through them or climb over them, and any attempt would surely leave visible damage."

There followed again a silence in our compartment, so I raised my next thought by saying, "It certainly looks, Holmes, as if you have a thoroughly convincing collection of reasons to justify your case against Reuben Healy. Is it not then time to go to Scotland Yard and let them find Reuben and charge him?"

Holmes hesitated, with a nervous smile. "No, Watson," he answered, "Scotland Yard is only interested in clear and unambiguous evidence. I have only a theory and the conclusions of my deductions to offer. I fear that their interest and enthusiasm for my work will be at best cautious. But who knows, if we visit Reuben Healy, we may learn more. Perhaps he will even betray himself if we ask him appropriately. Or perhaps, we might find a penitent sinner, relieved that he can tell us the truth!"

I nodded, but there was no time for more, as it was time to alight at London Bridge.

An unusual discovery

Despite the busy traffic in front of the London Bridge station, we succeeded quickly in securing a free hansom to bring us further. Our journey took us over London Bridge to the north bank. We then turned to the east, and the journey was not long, as our destination was Fenchurch Street station. As we arrived, a train to Blackwall was just leaving, but this was scarcely a concern, as the trains ran every fifteen minutes for the dockland workpeople. We spent a few minutes on the platform, where the appearance of many workmen obviously going to their jobs suggested that this was a changeover time for shifts of the dockworkers.

The train we were awaiting arrived from the docks, drawn by a diminutive locomotive with great whistling and noise of steam, and consisting of several small coaches. The little engine had no tender like its fellows on the main lines; here the distance to cover was short and the engines carried their own supplies in tanks and bunkers. That was not my concern. Although there was, according to the ticket clerk, supposed to be a first-class carriage, this was not to be found, but Holmes went on without concern and climbed aboard. This was my first experience of such a workmen's train. The hard wooden benches between the low wooden divider created a semblance of compartments, with doors on both sides. I must admit, dear readers, that though I know little of contemporary agriculture, I imagine that a chicken house on wheels would not be very different. Holmes climbed in, ducking his head, and sat at the window and door on the opposite side.

More workpeople climbed in, obviously surprised to see us in city clothes, and our train set off, again with steam and noise, for our short journey to the docks. Holmes seemed absorbed in thought. I looked round, and to the wooden ceiling, to see a small oil lamp, fixed in a kind of chimney, which would not have granted us much light in the winter darkness of east London. How depressing such a train must be in the depths of winter, late at night or in the early morning, how bitterly cold, and without any warmth or comfort. But now our train was stopping, as we reached a grey and dirty station, and more workmen climbed in. In the now well-filled compartment, where there was scarcely room between all our knees, those now entering had to look carefully as they put their feet on the carriage floor. This happened two or three times, as ever more men pressed into the little train.

Opposite me was an older man, truly unkempt, noisily chewing his wad of tobacco. Without going into detail, dear reader, it was obvious that these trains were conceived to be indifferent of muddy boots and dirty clothes. We were certainly out of place here, as showed itself as our fellow travellers were obviously exchanging opinions behind their hands, while watching us suspiciously. It was all the more obvious because among themselves the mood was cheerful and the air full of earthy expressions. I fear I was not at ease, and therefore relieved when after only twelve minutes the train reached Millwall Junction, where we alighted.

It may be that you have, dear reader, already made one of those most instructive visits to the London docks offered by the docks administration. If so, you will have seen for yourself something of the inconceivable variety and quantity of the goods involved in our British trade with our great Empire and, indeed, the whole world. Should that be so, you will forgive my short description of the world in which Holmes and I now found ourselves.

Between Limehouse and Blackwall, north of the Isle of Dogs, which is formed by a sharp bend of the River Thames, are the West India Docks. Some of the greatest steamship lines have their berths here, to unload and load their cargoes. Further upstream by Blackwall are the East India Docks, which are rather smaller. They are extensively used by sailing vessels. The Millwall Docks are on the Isle of Dogs, and therefore to the south of the West India Docks. We were to find the address of Reuben Healey, at The Ship's Wheel public house, and so had to go north from the station of Millwall Junction into the adjoining residential streets of the dockworkers.

Over the station there is a long footbridge, spanning an extensive net of rail tracks. This bridge offers a spectacular view of the docks, and of all the associated installations. Everywhere there are long buildings. These are the warehouses for storage of tea, coffee, sugar, timber, silk, tobacco and more, and many manufactories. I stared at the sight, and Holmes told me that many of the warehouses have also vaults to store wines and spirits. The warehouses were one feature; but everywhere were the dock basins themselves, the cranes and derricks, and quaysides, with everything needed to handle the cargoes passing in and out and all around the loading and unloading of ships. Everywhere were stacks of goods, barrels, bales, and crates, cargoes heaped up, and also the workpeople with nets and ropes, the railway wagons on the quaysides, and over everything smoke from the steam engines that gave their power to cranes and winches. I could scarcely take my eyes off it all, but Holmes was anxious to get on, and was already crossing the long bridge northwards.

The bridge brought us to where we could cross High Street and East India Dock Road, before turning into Kerby Street. We were now in a grey and forbidding quarter of dockworkers' dwellings, grim terraces of small brick houses, where even on this summer day the air seemed heavy and foul. The sun had given up any attempt to break through here. The atmosphere was not only grey but threatening. I was suddenly painfully aware that since the early morning, we had come far, and Baker Street was now geographically far away from us. I hoped inwardly that Holmes knew where to go. But before I could give voice to my doubts, he had already turned left into Market Street, and I saw at the next street corner a ship's wheel hanging over the pavement. Painted in garish colours, it told us that we had reached the public house known as The Ship's Wheel.

Holmes and I went inside. There were already three workmen at a long wooden table, their arms on the table and their heads bedded down in sleep. Perhaps they were exhausted from heavy work, perhaps they had already drunk too heavily, I would not know, as at that moment a corpulent figure appeared, and wiped his hands on a rather dirty apron, took a cloth in his hands, and said, "Come inside, gentlemen, there's a room at the back where you can be quieter. A good beer is just what you need on a day like today."

Holmes nodded approvingly, and so we found ourselves in the back room, which certainly gave a better impression of cleanliness than did the public bar. Before ordering his beer, Homes asked whether we were speaking with Mr. William Knox, the landlord.

"You are indeed, sir, that's me! But everyone here knows me as Sam."

"Certainly, then, Sam. My name is Sherlock Holmes, and this is my colleague Dr. Watson. We would like to ask you some questions."

As Holmes said this, the face of the landlord betrayed his instinctive suspicion. Holmes at once reassured him. "Please do not be alarmed. The questions I have do not concern you, but I assure you that your time will be well reimbursed."

As he spoke, Holmes took a half-sovereign from his waistcoat pocket, and laid it rather demonstratively on the table. Mr. Knox' looked less doubtful, and then said, "Well, sir, no promises, but if I can answer your questions, I will."

"Good, Sam, then first we need two tankards of your best, and please bring one for yourself. And then we will sit together, as it will make it easier to talk with one another."

Sam smiled and almost turned on his heel. However, having missed breakfast, and with only a small snack in the Crystal Palace, I thought it prudent to lay a better foundation before consuming Sam's beer. I asked, before he disappeared, "Sam, have you anything good to eat at this time of day?"

Sam stopped, and then said thoughtfully, "Well, there is still some of yesterday's ham and egg pie, sir."

"That sounds splendid," I replied, "then you may bring me a portion."

With this request he continued out to the public bar. A few minutes later we were sitting together, and Holmes began. "If I am not mistaken, I believe you have a certain Reuben Healy lodging here. Is that so?"

"Yes, that is so," he replied, rather unwillingly as it seemed. "But sir, what, if I may ask, has a gentleman like you to do with a layabout like Healy?"

"I do not know him personally, but my colleague here, Dr. Watson, asks me to assist him to obtain settlement of an account for a treatment some time ago, and for which Healy has so far failed to make the agreed payment."

I knew nothing of this, of course, and was almost overcome with the fragment of pie in my mouth. To avoid coughing, I struggled to remain calm, and this in turn brought tears to my eyes. Mr. Knox knew not the reason for my discomfort, and said with a sigh, and with proper sympathy, "Dr. Watson, I understand only too well. During the time he has lodged here, he has all too often failed to pay the rent, and this week is just the same. It's already Friday, the week's rent is due, and I have not seen him. Reuben is a difficult case. Either he loses his money at cards or betting, or he drinks himself insensible. I would have put him out long ago, but my wife, Ruth, stops me. I think Reuben reminds her of our son, lost years ago at sea. And I value my peace too much to argue."

Holmes discreetly changed the subject, without comment. "Does Reuben have a regular employment?"

"To be quite honest, sir, I cannot rightly say. I don't think so. When he first lodged here, he went out at six o'clock in the morning to take work in the docks, and as he is very strong, he seems to have been engaged here and there. But I understand that he lost that because he was always in arguments and even in a fight with his gang foremen."

"Would you know if he is now in his room?"

"I know he is not, Mr. Holmes."

"Really, Sam?"

"Yes, I would take a safe bet on it." Holmes said nothing, and Sam enlarged upon his remark. "Reuben lives upstairs, and the only way in and out is to go through the public bar. That's the only street door. The pub entrance is our front door. As soon as I lock it, no one else can come in or out. I keep the key. Reuben went out yesterday, and has since then not come back. He is certainly not in his room, and perhaps he has slept off his hangover somewhere on a street corner. It would not be the first time."

Here Mr. Knox broke off, and took a deep draft from his beer, before continuing, rather more agitatedly. "Mr. Holmes, Reuben was certainly very strange in these last days, and yesterday he was even worse."

"Was he now?" asked Holmes, apparently disinterested, although I knew he would be burning to know what the landlord would say next.

"I mean it, sir, he had slept late, and went out of the house here late in the morning. Around midday a lad came, with a packet from a laundry, addressed to Reuben. He simply said it was a delivery, everything was in order, and there was nothing more to pay. That being so, I took the packet, but it annoyed me that he could pay for laundry, but he couldn't pay my rent. Not only that, Ruth has always washed his things and there was never a word of thanks.

I gave him the parcel when he came back in the afternoon, and he went upstairs, but no sooner away was he back down here again, wanting the Evening News & Post. That is our evening paper, which Ruth and I like to read. I gave him the previous evening's edition, but no, he insisted it must be the newest edition, which I had hardly looked at. It seemed a real cheek on his part, but Ruth said I should humour him. I was hardly back in the public bar, but there came a telegraph boy with a telegram for Reuben. I sent him up to Reuben, he came down again. Some time went by, and then I heard Reuben run downstairs, past me, without a word, and slam the door as he went into the street. I have to say, Mr. Holmes, that I was pleased to see him go, and I don't want to have to see him again for a while."

If Sam were hoping for some consolation, it was not forthcoming. Rather, Holmes asked at once, whether we could see Reuben's room.

Sam was visibly reluctant, but the appearance of a second half-sovereign on the table seemed to reassure him. He smiled and said, "Well, gentlemen, I suppose so, come with me then."

He first took us upstairs to the first floor where he and him wife lived, disappeared for a moment and returned with an iron key. "That is the key to the loft where Reuben sleeps," he said, "but I must get back downstairs to the public bar. Just look at anything you like, and let me know when you are finished."

The room, which we now entered, was for me almost forbidding. The low sloping ceiling meant that one could hardly stand upright, and what furniture there was appeared simple and rude. Beyond this, however, the total disorder disturbed me deeply. Holmes had already started to search through in his usual manner, while I stood in the doorway and took in a view of the chaos which reigned. The bed was unmade, and on the floor lay scattered items of obviously dirty clothes; there were some fragments of broken glass; and there was a screwed-up scrap of paper.

On the table was the parcel from the laundry, which had obviously contained a nightshirt. With it was the open evening paper, and an almost empty bottle of hard liquor. I well understood what the landlord had meant, as he said, he was pleased not to have to meet Reuben Healy again, in such a wild state as earlier. I was also only too anxious not to have to confront him, this drunken, unpredictable, and unusually strong man, and yet here we were, searching through his bedroom. I found myself listening, in case he should suddenly come back to the public house. If so, I would try to warn Holmes, so that we could take cover, though I knew not where.

Holmes finished off his search on the floor and came to me. "Look what we have here!" he said, with an agitated voice, holding up the paper, which I had seen screwed up on the floor. It was a telegram, dispatched from Sydenham, and it contained the following message:

Reuben - I saw you. I know. We must speak. Tonight 9 o'clock Crystal Palace. - Joseph

When I had read it, I told Holmes, "Miss Hooper told us she had seen Joseph, lost in thought, at the Telegraph Office. He had surely just sent this telegram."

"Quite, Watson, and it is a most important piece of evidence, for it confirms our suspicion that Reuben was Joseph's murderer. Now I have something definite, with which I can go to Scotland Yard, and on which they must act."

I shared Holmes' opinion, and reflected, that Reuben was perhaps not sleeping off his drunkenness, but already trying to get away. Holmes thought, and replied, "It could well be so,

Watson. He may even have drunk himself insensible, and then realised what he had done. But now it is the task of Lestrade and Gregson to act, because with their resources they have a much better chance than we of finding him"

"So now we are going to Scotland Yard?"

"Yes, Watson, but first we must finish our work here. I want to study this nightshirt more closely."

I could not think why, but I followed him to the table. Holmes took the nightshirt, held it up, unfolded it and examined it with his glass. He was murmuring, more to himself than to me.

"This nightshirt is of a much better quality than everything else lying here. It doesn't seem to have been worn, so why was it at the laundry? And it is surely much too small for a man like Reuben. That is all very curious."

Now he turned the shirt inside out and looked at the material again with his magnifying glass, just where the right sleeve was attached. At once he stopped sharply and turned to me with a triumphant expression. "Eureka," he exclaimed, loudly, giving me the glass and letting me look. There was pinned inside the sleeve a small piece of paper. It did not seem too exciting, for laundries often attach such notes. Holmes however took it from me, released the pin and unfolded the paper. It had on it the following sequence of letters.

DITTL AOGHO WITHT ELEID UTREX NIAEF RNDSI GUAIF SANSS

I saw how Holmes's eyes lit up, and for a moment a nervous smile came to his lips. He then took the slip of paper, putting it most carefully into his pocket-book. He then examined the brown paper of the parcel. There was no address of any laundry. Reuben's address was written in rather clumsy capital letters, apparently with a rather blunt pencil. There was also an irregular arrow, beside the address, which might have suggested that the parcel was urgent. When Holmes had finished his examination, he put the wrapping paper beside the nightshirt on the table. Then he said, "Come Watson, now there is nothing else of importance here."

They left the room, turned the key and went downstairs, where Sam was standing at his bar. Holmes gave him the key, and the promised payment, and said, "Thank you, Sam. I think it would be better not to tell Mr. Healy of our visit."

With this, he took another half-sovereign from his waistcoat pocket, and offered it to Sam. The landlord took it gratefully, and said with a smile, "At your service, gentlemen."

He stepped quickly to the door, opened it for us and saw us into the street. As we left, he bowed slightly and wished us a very pleasant day. I hoped indeed that it might be so, but we still had to make the return journey in the workmen's train, on the Blackwall Railway, by which we had come. That was a prospect which did not please me.

How various threads came together

I would, dear reader, not fatigue you with too many details of our journey to Scotland Yard. It was for me strenuous, certainly because we had now been at work much of the day, and the London weather was again very hot. Holmes seemed not to notice it. As we left The Ship's Wheel, he sank into a deep silence. Only moments later, it seemed, he suddenly broke his silence, but said nothing about our case, regaling me with a description and comparison of musical instruments, which, I fear, lay at a considerably higher level than my musical knowledge could support.

Once in Scotland Yard, we were able after a short wait to see Inspector Gregson. Holmes described briefly our progress and told him of our suspicion that Reuben was the murderer. Holmes told him how the deed needed a very strong person, who was also familiar with the Crystal Palace Park and its maze, and who must have been known to the victim, since they could not have otherwise gone together to the centre of the labyrinth. Finally, he described, without reference to the missing thumb, how the murderer had to have been left-handed, and that this was so with Reuben Healy. Inspector Gregson listened to my friend, as it appeared, more politely than out of real interest. When, however, Holmes showed him the telegram, his manner changed abruptly, and he exclaimed,

"But that is excellent, Mr. Holmes. It has every appearance of a settlement between brothers, and Reuben Healy has surely fled. He cannot remain long at large, however, as I will initiate an official police search. Lestrade will be green with envy, when I am able to conclude the affair before he does."

Saying this, he was rubbing his hands in anticipation. Holmes however then began to describe the note in the nightshirt in the laundry parcel, but Gregson showed no interest in it. He merely glanced at it and remarked,

"I do not think that scrap of paper has any interest for us. The photograph of Hooper's Grocer's shop is, however, of great interest, and I would be pleased to retain it. Reuben Healy is, as you say, illustrated on it, and I can use it therefore to give a better description."

Holmes said nothing but put the small note from the laundry back into his notebook and took out the photograph to give to the Inspector. I saw Gregson's face fall, as he realised that the small image on the photograph would perhaps not yield the detail he had hoped. I therefore added helpfully, "But it is apparent that he is a most powerfully built young man, as Holmes has already said. Moreover, Healy's arms are covered with tattoos, and we know that he has lost his right thumb. These details should also help you in your search."

Gregson's expression turned at once to resignation. He sighed deeply and said, in a bitterly disappointed voice, as he put the photograph aside, "Your description is good, so good, indeed, that I can now tell you that we have already found Reuben Healy."

I looked in complete surprise at Inspector Gregson, and I saw that Holmes had also raised his eyebrows. Gregson began, quietly, to explain. "Do you recall, gentlemen, that I had a telegram this morning from Inspector Lestrade?"

"Of course," I said with some irritation.

Gregson continued.

"Your description of Reuben Healy corresponds perfectly to the corpse which was found in the early morning in the Thames. Admittedly, it had been again disfigured, almost certainly by a steam launch passing over it, so that at first I could not make much of it. It is the elaborate tattoo on the arms, and the missing thumb, which are however decisive. I now suspect that Reuben Healy had committed the crime in a state of high drunkenness, and then later realised what he had done, so that he then went and took his own life. That would be a convincing admission of guilt."

We remained all very quiet. The inspector's words seemed then quite unreal as he added, "The suicide of Reuben Healy is certainly regrettable, as I would dearly have wished to arrest him and show the absurdity of Lestrade's theory. On the other hand, the police have been saved a great deal of effort in finding Healy. I am in any case most grateful to you, Mr. Holmes, and of course to you, Dr. Watson, for all your efforts to clear up this affair."

With this it was apparent that Gregson considered the conversation at an end, and he wished us, with some finality, a pleasant day, explaining that he had some urgent preparations for the openingof the new Tower Bridge by the Prince of Wales, an event which would be a major affair of state.

On our way back to Baker Street, Holmes remained silent. My attempt to speak to him was ignored. I shared Gregson's view that the matter was now concluded, and that it was time to close the file. However, I knew that would not be Holmes' view. I knew him too well, and I was sure that he was not ready to give it up. He would apply all his energies to finding out what the confused letters on the note might mean. I had also felt that the letters were, for a laundry note, rather unusual, but there was surely nothing of a secret behind them. However, not wishing to distract Holmes even more, I kept my opinion to myself.

I also wished to avoid being caught up in Holmes' bad mood, if he should try to decipher the letters and fail to find anything. I knew that he would carry on by trial and error to overcome any number of disappointments, before he admitted that there really was no hidden message. I did therefore the best I could think of, and said, "Holmes, I am going now to my Regimental Club, for the remainder of the afternoon to relax. If you have no other plans, I will take dinner there too."

Holmes only nodded and muttered something, so, since I had not understood him, I assumed he was in agreement. There was no more time to talk, as we were already in Baker Street and alighting at 221B. Holmes jumped down agilely as always, and closed the cab door, leaving me to go on alone.

My first objective was, however, not my club, but the Turkish bath on Northumberland Avenue. Here I could let body and mind be released from the extraordinary intensity of impressions they had suffered since the early morning. Perhaps I also wished to remove any remaining traces of the insalubrious workmen's train on the Blackwall line.

I was back in Baker Street by nine o'clock, perhaps earlier than intended because I had a rather disturbed conscience, having left Holmes so abruptly. I found him, as I expected, at the table, writing. The table and the floor were covered by scraps of paper, screwed up and thrown carelessly away. I announced that I was back, and he looked at me in surprise, to say, to my complete astonishment, "Back? Were you away then?"

There was no answer to this, so I gave none. He however simply turned back to his papers, and to the task I had obviously interrupted. I resolved therefore to sit comfortably in my armchair in front of the fireplace, and read further in my poetry book, until it was time to go to bed. In that way I could accompany him, although he probably attached no importance to that. Even so, my conscience could not allow me to leave him alone with such an obviously demanding problem.

I had in fact gone to sleep when I felt a firm grip on my shoulder. I awoke with a start, to find Holmes leaning over me. A satisfied smile and a brightness in his eye showed me that he had something to tell me. I tried to think clearly. My book was on the floor, my neck was stiff.

"Sorry, Holmes, I must have nodded off, what time is it?"

"Just before midnight, old friend".

"My goodness, I should be going to bed. Holmes, good night". I came no further, for he broke in with, "I have decoded the message sent to Reuben Healy."

"What have you done? A message?"

"Yes, Watson, the strip of paper which you probably held to be a control label of the laundry, contained a coded message. Would you like to know what it says?" His voice was so charged that suddenly any tiredness was away.

With a new interest and with a measure of unbelief, I had to say, "But of course, Holmes."

"Then sit here while I explain."

I sat beside him, and he first started to explain how he had solved it. I suspect that if I had shown no interest, he would have been hurt, and perhaps said no more. I had no other choice than, as so often with him, to be patient.

He began slowly. "If you have carefully read my monograph on codes and decoding, you will know that there are two main families of codes, those of substitution, and those of transposition. One can also combine them in practice, which makes the task of decoding certainly far more difficult. In substitution, each letter may be replaced by another of the alphabet. With transposition, the message remains as before, but the letters and components are, in accordance with an agreed secret system, ordered differently." He looked at me.

"The coded message on the paper consists of nine words, or at least, nine groups of letters. It is also short, which makes the decoding more difficult. I tried unsuccessfully with substitution methods, but at length tried a transposition approach, which led me into possible solutions. You will see that each group contains five letters. This suggested that a matrix approach might be better." Here he took a piece of paper and drew on it a matrix with nine columns and five lines.

"It looks like a chess board," I remarked with new curiosity. "Presumably the letter groups should be put in the columns."

"Quite so, Watson, try it out yourself."

Holmes grinned and gave me a pencil. He pushed over towards me the paper with the matrix, and the strip of paper from Reuben Healy's laundry. The task was quickly done and so my work appeared as here shown.

D	A	W	E	U	N	R	G	S
I	O	I	L	T	I	N	U	A
T	G	T	E	R	A	D	A	N
T	H	H	I	E	E	S	I	S
L	O	T	D	X	F	I	F	S

When I had finished, I recall that I sighed, raised my eyebrows and remarked, "I'm sorry, Holmes, it still does not make sense."

"Ah, Watson, that is because you do not know how the matrix should be used. I tried out several approaches, before I suddenly remembered the paper in which the nightshirt was packed."

I understood nothing, and at my stare he continued, somewhat agitated, "Do you not recall, Watson, that on the label, at the side of the address of Healy, there was an arrow, pointing in a spiral downwards?"

Vaguely I did and was even more confused.

"That arrow, Watson, defined the way in which you should move through the matrix. The first letters to be used are thus DAITOWEIG and so on."

I interrupted him, a little annoyed, to say, "But Holmes, that still makes no sense."

"Quite so, Watson, because the columns of the matrix are still in complete disorder. When we discover the proper order, we will find the message."

I looked at him in dismay to ask, "But how should we know how to do that?"

He smiled again, and then pulled out, from under the pile of sheets of paper which he had been using, a copy of a newspaper. I saw at once that it was a rather ill-treated copy of yesterday's Evening News and Post, and I realised that it gave off a not entirely pleasant, if not disagreeable, smell.

"Where did you get that?" I asked in surprise.

"I asked Mrs. Hudson to obtain a copy for me, from the neighbours, but she had not even to leave the house; this morning's herrings had been wrapped up in it."

I could not avoid laughing, for at least this explained the smell, but what came next? "What had then a newspaper from the fishmonger to add to the solution of our problem?"

"Everything, Watson. As soon as the landlord of The Ship's Wheel told us that Reuben Healy had demanded, so categorically, that this edition of the Evening News and Post was what he wanted, my curiosity was provoked. I have studied the newspaper, especially the page which was open in Healy's room, and under the heading of 'Personal' I found the following short announcement." He gave me the newspaper, with his finger on the personal message. It read,

RH: We expect you tomorrow in EDINBURGH

I look at Holmes questioningly.

"The key word which tells us how to order the matrix is EDINBURGH. First, we convert it into a numerical form.

Each letter of the word takes the number of its order of appearance in the alphabet. Thus the b in *Edinburgh* takes number 1. Looking again, the 'd' is numbered 2. Doing this with all the letters gives us a series, 326719845. In this process, the key word must have a sufficient diversity of letters, for otherwise there would be confusion. Now we will write again the nine groups of letters of the strip of paper."

I did as he said and obtained

DITTL AOGHO WITHT ELEID UTREX NIAEF RNDSI
1 2 3 4 5 6 7
GUAIF SANSS
8 9

"Now draw a new matrix and enter in it the letter groups again, but this time not in the earlier numerical order, but as in the same order as the numbers from our code word. 326719845." I did so, and obtained the following table:

W	A	N	R	D	S	G	E	U
I	O	I	N	I	A	U	L	T
T	G	A	D	T	N	A	E	R
H	H	E	S	T	S	I	I	E
T	O	F	I	L	S	F	D	X

"Excellent, Watson. If you now go through the matrix as the arrow directed us, you may write down the resulting series of letters."

Feeling a little more confident, I did so, and obtained the following series:

WAITONRIGHTHANDSIDEOFSTAGEUNTILSALUTEIS FIRED

Before I could, open-mouthed, react, Holmes spoke again. "See, Watson, you have done it! The message is,

WAIT ON RIGHTHAND SIDE OF STAGE UNTIL SALUTE IS FIRED.

He continued, "For persons using the code, the work of coding and decoding is made easier with this grouping. Anyone not knowing the code has however in this last regrouping a further obstacle to overcome, because loss of the separation of the words forming the message conceals the sense right up to the last moment."

I was truly amazed and surprised as I looked at my friend and back at the decoded note. I felt almost like applauding, but I was nevertheless aware that Holmes was correct – we had decoded the message on that small scrap of paper, certainly a secret well-concealed, but we were still, as far as I could see, no wiser than before. As I said so, Holmes was then again in full concentration.

"Indeed, Watson, this message looks at first to be quite harmless. We must therefore ask ourselves why it was in code, for that suggests that it is indeed a matter of importance. The fact that it refers to a stage, and to a salute being fired, suggests a significant public event. I believe we can deduce what this might be. Tomorrow is the inauguration of the new bridge, Tower Bridge, which will be a major public event. I am inclined to suspect that an attack is planned to harm our country at the highest level. It will be directed upon the public figures, the Prince of Wales and his guests, who will be participating."

I looked at him, suddenly appalled at the significance of his words. This was a dreadful suspicion. He began to explain, in his characteristic way.

"Everything that I am now taking into account has come to us in the course of our investigations into the murder of Joseph Healy.

"We know that Joseph Healy, as future son-in-law of the owner of Hooper's grocery and provisions store in Sydenham, spent much of his time there. Beyond that, he worked for the fireworks company C.T. Brock & Co., and was responsible for the firework displays at the Crystal Palace, as also for the great firework display to follow the inauguration of Tower Bridge.

"On finding the telegram, which Joseph Healy had sent to his brother Reuben, we learned that Joseph had seen something which in his opinion demanded that they meet at once.

"Let us first ask ourselves the *where?* and *why?* behind this observation of Joseph's. We already knew that Joseph had only left Sydenham to go to the site of the next display, at

Tower Bridge. We also heard that the fireworks for the display were stored in a warehouse nearby. Miss Hooper told us that Joseph was still occupied with the display at the Crystal Palace, as he had spent the last few days preparing for the Tower Bridge display. I therefore concluded that Joseph had seen his brother either at Tower Bridge or in the nearby docks."

He paused, and interrupted his account to offer me a cigarette from his silver case, as he drew one for himself. He then continued, "Now let us address another item which may not have seemed important at the time, as we studied the murder, but which was even then curious. This was the theft of the enamel panel with the advertising message of the firework specialists of C.T. Brock & Co., and also the observation that six wooden firework crates were missing. We know that these losses affected Joseph Healy, so that he was greatly concerned. Now, I may be mistaken, but I suggest that strong wooden crates, which are used for carrying fireworks, are also ideally suited to the transport of dynamite and fuses. And a waggon with an advertising panel for the company providing the firework display would have no difficulty in gaining access, to the vicinity of the stages which had been erected for the guests."

As Holmes paused again, my thoughts raced to catch up with him. "You think then that Reuben Healy was involved in a plot to make an attack on the inauguration, and that his brother had suspected that this was so?"

Holmes nodded, and so I carried on with my thought. "And Joseph had sent the telegram to speak to his brother and to try to prevent any such fearful act?"

"Quite so, Watson. We know that the brothers were very different, but that Joseph had always taken responsibility for his brother. He had however shown Reuben that there were limits. That we saw in the incidents of drunkenness during his employment as watchman at the Crystal Palace, and also with the thefts from the shop in Sydenham. Then, it was certainly a painful experience for Reuben to be rejected, as he was, by Miss Hooper, and we know that Joseph would not give Reuben money, but insisted on paying Reuben's debts directly to Mr. Knox at The Ship's Wheel. It may be that, although his brother only wanted to protect him, Reuben, who was now involved in a far bigger matter than he had ever known, felt that his brother was a constant source of irritation and frustration. That was surely a bad start to the conversation, which did indeed take place in the maze at the Palace."

I could not stay silent. "Reuben in a wild fit of rage attacked his brother and slit his throat. This crime was gruesome, and we may well believe that Reuben, after he realised what he had done, set an end to his own life."

Holmes had again nodded, but then said at the end, "In view of the company which Reuben was keeping, made up of unscrupulous persons ready to inflict a most murderous attack, we may consider that Reuben's death was more probably not of his own free will. This is no band of common criminals or blackmailers. I fear here an attack which comes from plotters charged with destabilising once again the relations between states."

I looked at Holmes as he explained his remark. "He was not clever. He might have annoyed them in so many ways. He might have asked for money to leave London. But he was a risk. He had been given a key to the plotters' complex code. That meant that when he had done his allotted task, he could not in any case be allowed to survive. I know that when criminals at that level feel someone is a danger or an encumbrance, they do not hesitate to dispose of them. If an attack is planned as I fear, it will be an affair of state. Reuben was not in that class. I have no further knowledge which might help us."

We sat a while side by side, until I again thought of what was to come. We had to talk about the plans for the following day, with the possibility of an attack upon the Tower Bridge opening ceremony.

"What can we do now, Holmes?" It was a while before Holmes spoke again. He was weighing his words carefully.

"My suspicions of an attack are too vague to take to Scotland Yard," he said, "and their first reaction would be to doubt my concern. Even if they believed my reasoning, it is too late to take effective action there. What I can do is to go to Mycroft and tell him. He will know whatever is already known, of any potential threats, who might be at risk and what measures of national security have already been put in place. I think it best to go directly to him and tell him what we have discovered. When he is satisfied, he can act very quickly."

I listened approvingly. Mycroft Holmes was certainly in a position to act very quickly. As we knew, and Holmes always said, Mycroft, incisive and brilliant, was not only in the civil service to work for the government; sometimes it was apparent that, behind the scenes, Mycroft *was* the government. Mycroft is however a man of very fixed habits and conducts his personal life within strict limits, and he dislikes disturbances. He would not appreciate being disturbed for nothing.

"Shall I come with you, Holmes?" I asked.

"Good old Watson, always ready to act! It is very generous that you offer, but I think not. I am not certain that he will even listen to me, or even then, how much time he will give me, and I consider it more useful that you at least get some sleep before tomorrow. Whatever Mycroft thinks or does, I will be there tomorrow at the opening ceremony, and I intend to observe everything that happens. I think to find myself, perhaps with the aid of a well-filled purse, a window seat in one of the dwellings along the river, and there I would be pleased if you would accompany me. Would you do so?"

"Of course, Holmes," I agreed spontaneously.

He smiled briefly, but there was no concealing that he was prepared for desperate action if needed. But now he took up all that he wanted to show Mycroft, stuffed his pockets full and ran down the stairs, as I called to him with my good wishes.

The threat of disaster

When Holmes had left, I did not in fact go directly to bed, but first took a hansom to Kensington. There, in my study, I unlocked the drawer of my desk and took out my old Army revolver. If Homes were right in his suspicions, it was certainly not out of place to take it with me. I always kept it clean, but now I cleaned it and prepared it with particular care. Once ready, I put it in my jacket pocket and again took a hansom to return to Baker Street. I noted on entering that Holmes was not yet back, and went to my own room, where I fell into an exhausted but disturbed sleep.

Next morning, I was awakened by Mrs. Hudson, who told me that Holmes had not come home during the night. She brought a hearty breakfast, and then told me that he had indeed looked in, two hours earlier, to change his clothes and to give her some instructions. These had included waking me in good time, and giving me breakfast, and to tell me when to leave the house to go to an address which Holmes had given her. All this she did, and thus I was soon ready to go, summoning a cab to take me to Lower Thames Street.

There I stood at the house door at the address he had given me and took in my hand the impressive bell pull. A short pause followed, before the door was opened, and a young servant asked me politely after my business. Not having any better idea what we were to do, I said, "My name is Dr. Watson. My friend Sherlock Holmes asked me to come here."

It seemed that this was the correct approach, for the servant invited me in and asked me to follow. I was led to a salon on the second floor, and I was relieved to see that my friend was standing there at the window. He turned, smiled and said, "Good morning, Watson, I see that Mrs. Hudson has perfectly carried out my instructions."

Then, again, he was completely serious and took out a small retractable telescope from the coffee table, in order to study the scene before the window. Since the servant had now discreetly withdrawn, I asked him the question which had most concerned me.

"Did Mycroft take seriously your suspicion of an attack on the ceremony?"

"Yes, Watson, he most certainly did," replied Holmes, to my great relief. He told me how Mycroft had sent word at once to Superintendent William Melville.

He explained quickly that Superintendent Melville, the expert in his field, would know exactly what was involved. He was not only responsible, with his specialist team, for the safety of the foreign dignitaries during their stay but organised also the permanent protection of members of the Royal Family. He had carried out innumerable raids upon clubs and meeting rooms known for housing persons of anarchist convictions or showing suspicious behaviour. He had also suppressed and closed down agencies that print and circulate the pamphlets which such anarchists attempt to distribute. He knew many of the persons on whom suspicion rests, and had authority to act decisively when there is need. Superintendent Melville may already have known something, He might even have had suspicions of the perpetrators of such atrocities, but that must remain his secret. His men had already searched the bridge and the stage, but he was ready to do so again, both with his own agents and, in addition, with our friends Gregson and Lestrade from Scotland Yard under his orders.

Holmes was again silent, laid down the telescope and rubbed his eyes. I remarked, "I can well imagine that those two are not really pleased at these arrangements."

Holmes smiled, and he commented, "That was already clear to me this morning. The situation has however its advantages, as the two seem to have made peace in order to work together, rather than in competition. How long this will last is not sure, but for us there is surely an advantage." He was again silent and took up the telescope. I quickly asked, "How can a truce between those two be useful to us?"

"For a start, because my request to Superintendent Melville, that I might interrogate one of the attackers when they are apprehended, was, as I feared, refused outright. Lestrade and Gregson heard this, and discreetly offered to help me to find an opportunity. I want to find out about the people behind this affair, especially when they use intelligent codes, in their messages, which were worthy of the late Professor Moriarty, but also use people like Reuben Healy."

The hairs stood up on my neck as I heard the name of the now long-dead Moriarty. What was he thinking? I changed the subject.

"Was it confirmed that a dynamite charge is indeed involved?"

"It was indeed, Watson, and I believe I even won the respect of Superintendent Melville in this connection, though he naturally could not show it. In the following early hours, his men searched the whole site again, and, in all discretion, with particular attention to the stage and tribune. They finally found enough hidden dynamite to reduce the entire wooden stage to matchwood, and Superintendent Melville showed how thoughtful he is. He did not have the dynamite removed, but he ordered that the fuses were cut through, so that detonation is not possible. Having prevented the attack, he obviously hopes to catch red-handed the attacker who is charged with setting the fuses. What happens now, we will have to see. The whole affair is now safely in the hands of higher authority. We two are relieved of responsibility. We are sworn to silence, and I do not now expect to learn more."

After this explanation, he was again silent, and took up the telescope. Something in his mood displayed his sudden alertness. Although for me it was difficult to pick out details, I also looked out. Here, on the Thames, there was always a buzz of activity, almost as if it were Oxford Street. Now there were more and more small boats, and spectators, from both sides of the river. It was hard to see all that was going on, and my attention now turned to the great bridge itself. I had read the description by a reporter from "The Times," who had laid emphasis on the remarkable engineering achievement which the bridge represented.

The rapid growth of London's population, and of its trade and business, had meant that the traffic of the East End had also grown rapidly. A further river crossing east of London Bridge was clearly desirable but could not be realised without regard for the river traffic of all the ships serving the docks at this point. A new bridge could not be allowed to interfere with the river traffic and the navigation. One possibility might have been to build a very high bridge, but this would have been very unsightly, and the steep approaches would have been too much for the many horses engaged in all kinds of traffic in London's daily business.

The choice fell then on a bridge with a moving centre section, and this was achieved, after eight years, by building a bridge with two lifting sections, called bascules, allowing sailing ships to pass with their masts in place, and steamships to pass with their masts and high funnels. You may, dear reader, already have seen the bridge, and if so, I beg you to forgive the following details, should they seem wearying.

Looking at the bridge, the two towers are certainly the dominant feature. They rest on foundations deep in the rock under the river. The towers have been built in the neo-gothic architectural style, which harmonises admirably with the nearby Tower of London. This is however only external; the structure is a massive steel construction, which is clad in limestone and granite from Cornwall. The next which the observer sees are the huge chains on each side, and the footways connecting the top of the towers, which allow pedestrians to cross the bridge even when it is fully open to river traffic. These footbridges are reached within the towers either by staircases, or by use of the lifts.

The most interesting part of the bridge is formed, of course, by the two lifting bascules, with their operating mechanism. The bridge is opened and closed by two steam-powered machines, built by Armstrong Mitchell and Co. in Newcastle on Tyne. The operation takes only ninety seconds. Four large steam boilers are concealed in the southern tower. These supply the energy for the steam engines, of 360 horsepower, which, for the opening of the bridge, pump water up from the Thames to operate the lifting mechanism. This water, under pressure, suffices also to operate the lifts in the towers. On this morning, as I sat with Holmes at the window, I did not know this but as I wrote this account, I was determined to find out more.

It was time to direct our attention again from the great bridge to the activities around it. The tribune, with a centre stage, had been built as a bridge between the wall of the Tower of London and the bridge tower on the north side of the river. It was decorated with flags and flowers. The many official guests, and guests of honour, were not yet in their places, but the crowds of spectators were now quite dense. But now I heard suddenly a cheer, which spread around, as the carriage of Edward, Prince of Wales, and his lady, Alexandra of Denmark arrived. I watched fascinated as other carriages drove up, and the noble guests, some from abroad, filled up the tribune. Holmes, however, had obviously seen something which aroused his curiosity. I heard him murmur, “Now what is that small steamboat doing there?”

There were many steamboats, and I asked Holmes what he meant. “Look, Watson, under the bridge on our side, a small steam launch has just moored. A man has gone ashore and is vigorously waving his straw hat as if to signal to someone on the opposite bank”.

He shifted his position to look at the other bank. “Ah,” he breathed, “I have found the man on the other side, and he too is using a telescope.” Satisfied with this, Holmes turned back to the man with the straw hat. “He has joined in the crowd, but I think he has left the steamboat with steam up. Now he has disappeared in the crowd.”

Quite suddenly, there was the sharp shock and loud noise of an explosion. The noise of the crowd stopped abruptly, and then broke into agitated questions and answers. Smoke and flames arose from the small steamboat, but help was at once at hand, and the fire was quickly under control. This brief moment of shock was over as quickly as it had started, and the crowd turned its attention again to the ceremony being prepared.

I was relieved that this moment had passed over without more disturbance, and that obviously nobody had been hurt. Then I heard a detonation and realised that the artillery salute was already being fired.

I heard Holmes saying, “Remarkable, quite excellent. That was a perfect diversion.”

“Diversion?” I asked.

“Yes. Watson, while all were distracted by the burning boat under the bridge, the man with the straw hat made his way, unobserved, nearer to the stage. The shots of the salute were his signal to light the fuses, and then I saw how he reappeared at the back of the stage and could merge again into the crowd. Melville’s men have missed him.”

I waited nervously the next turn of events. If the Superintendent’s men had successfully cut all the fuses, we were safe, but if not, we might experience a much more destructive explosion. The tension was acute, but as the next minutes ticked away, we were relieved that nothing had happened. The moment had now come where the Prince of Wales was to turn a large shining handle, and open the bridge with ceremony, before he went to the steps leading down from his seat on the stage, to walk with his escorts to a lower level. At that moment there was another incident. Events occurred faster than I could follow. A young man sprang up, to step towards where the Prince was descending, but before he could reach him, he was seized by four strong bodyguards who appeared as if from nowhere. I turned, quite shocked, to Holmes.

“Did you see that?”

"I did indeed, Watson, and it shows what we had feared. These people had, for reasons we do not know, not only prepared an elaborate plot with explosives, but had a reserve for the case that the explosion of the dynamite might not work as planned. They had an armed man, ready to make a murderous and even suicidal attack. That might have been Reuben's job – remember the coded message. If the dynamite had exploded, this gang member must have died too. Superintendent Melville obviously expected the desperate attempt and was ready with his men to make the arrest in good time. The Prince of Wales, surely warned in advance, was never in danger, and few will have noticed the incident. We may yet learn, from this man whom they have apprehended and what is behind this whole affair."

As he spoke, he clearly had a sudden thought. He turned, took up the telescope, and searched again in the crowd. He muttered to himself, "I thought so, the man we saw there on the south side is one of them and is still watching with the crowd. Now that the plot has failed, he will surely disappear into the crowd, discreetly because he will expect that there are agents there too. Then, after a few minutes, without attracting attention, he can make his escape."

He put the telescope in his pocket and called, "Come, Watson, we might yet catch him if we are quick, now!"

He crossed the salon with quick strides and ran downstairs to the street. There were still crowds of spectators, which gave me a moment to catch him up as we found our way out. I ran after him as well as I could. I called, despite the noise, "How are we to get across, now that the bridge is open?"

"We will go through the Tower Subway!" he answered sharply.

The Tower Subway is a Tunnel, which was built in 1870 by Barlow, and runs under the Thames from the foot of Great Tower Hill to Southwark. It consists of a metal tube, 1,263 feet in length, and 6 feet 6 inches in diameter. At first there was a carriage on rails to carry people in a small wagon, that accommodated 10 persons, drawn backwards and forwards by a steel cable with small steam winches at each end, and taking only 70 seconds for the trip. This was unpopular and was soon abandoned. The tunnel thus became a footway.

We soon reached the small tower at the north entrance. We descended as fast as we could the spiral staircase with its 96 steps, and I noticed that it was in a most disreputable condition.

As we reached the tunnel itself, we saw a long tube disappearing before us, and no end to be seen. It seemed misty. There were lamps, but their light was dim and did not reach far. The tunnel walls were damp. The boards under our feet felt irregular and unsteady, like walking on the deck of a ship. Holmes rushed ahead of me, and I had difficulty in following. We were fortunately alone in the tunnel, for passing would have been difficult, and even walking alone the tube felt very narrow and confining. Walking in the middle, there was scarcely room to walk upright.

When I estimated that we must be half-way, it was very quiet, as in the catacombs. An obsessive feeling of "How far have we still to go?" took hold of me, and it would have been easy to panic. Suddenly, in the quiet, I heard a beating noise. It was the paddle wheels of a steamer over my head. My imagination saw the depth of dirty river water over our heads, which at the first fault would pour in on us. My heart hammered, and my breath was fearful and rapid. An effort of will brought my feelings again under control. In the hope that this torment would soon end, I tried to keep up with Holmes as he disappeared into the darkness before us.

There was the spiral staircase to climb out. We had reached the end. There were still 96 steps to climb, and struggle as I might, to reach the light and the sunshine, I was out of breath. I could not keep up with Holmes. My leg reminded me at every step of my old Afghan wound.

When I reached daylight, we had already taken several minutes. Were we wasting our time, too late? There was no sign of Holmes. I ran as best I could towards where the man had been standing in the crowd, when Holmes first spotted him. The crowds were still dense, on the river bank, and perhaps he was not far away. I ran along Pickle Herring Street, looking up every dark side street and alley. In Horselydown Lane I was in luck. There I glimpsed Holmes, as he turned left. We were not too late, for I saw he was chasing a man, whom he had nearly caught. I expected Holmes to leap on him from behind, to bring him down. But Holmes suddenly stopped in mid-stride and fell forwards. I stared at his still body and cried

“No!” In my anguish, I felt how fear take hold of my heart and freeze my thinking. I had to drive myself to think, and as my mind worked again, I saw the fugitive run towards the end of the street, where a cab stood, as if awaiting a fare. The driver was, however, not looking to his horse, but back down the street. He had something in his hand, and only then in the distance could I see that it was a weapon.

I had heard no shot, as Holmes fell, but I could no longer be sure what was real, and what was the pounding of my heart, reflecting my fear. But now, as Holmes lay on the floor, the fugitive stopped, turned and walked back towards Holmes. I was shocked into action. Whether or not Holmes lived, no evildoer was to come near him, and for that I would risk my own life. I took my army revolver and fired two shots at the man as he approached Holmes as if to kick him. It was scarcely possible at this distance to hit him, or indeed the cab driver, but I could surely draw them away from Holmes.

My two shots hit something metallic, for beside the sound of the shot there was a clang, which set the dogs in the vicinity barking. Fortunately, this street, further from the river, was empty, but, whether or not they heard the shots, people here were clearly not curious. It seemed that at least my desperate measure had succeeded, for the unknown man beside Holmes looked quickly up at me, and then ran to the hansom, whose driver was controlling his horse only with difficulty after my two shots. As soon as our fugitive was inside and closing the door, the horse was whipped up and set off furiously. The cab swung recklessly round a corner and disappeared. I ran as fast as my legs would carry me, to be beside Holmes.

I knelt beside him, and still unconsciously holding my revolver, I reached out to press on his throat. I can hardly even now describe the joy of realising that there was a pulse, weak but regular. There was at first no obvious wound but turning his head I saw blood running from a wound on his temple. It was clear that the wound was superficial, not damaging the bone, but the impact, on a such sensitive spot, had surely knocked him out. I eased his collar, and within a minute or so he opened his eyes and saw me at first with difficulty.

"What has happened? What about my head?" he asked in some confusion.

"You were following someone who was running away. His partner took a shot at you, but it only touched you lightly. The two villains then made their escape in their own hansom."

I saw how he gradually recovered his senses, and that his memory was coming back. As he sat up, with a groan, he lifted a hand to his wound.

He wanted to stand up but was still unsteady. I secured my revolver, put it in my pocket and offered him my hand. I had forgotten the weapon, but Holmes saw it, and smiled weakly and said, "It was good that you brought it. Have you used it?"

"Yes, Holmes," I assured him grimly, "but with modest success."

As I said this, Holmes struggled to his feet, and stood somewhat unsteadily, holding my arm.

"Watson, you should not attempt to hide your light under a bushel. You did well. But not a word to the police about this incident here. The man we were chasing is most certainly one of the plotters and is clearly involved in the attempt to murder the Prince of Wales and his guests. We do not know who they are, or what they hoped to achieve, but they have no scruples, and will stop at nothing. This is already a serious business, Watson. Superintendent Melville has a big task on his hands. And we must say nothing." The street was still suspiciously empty.

Holmes' generous words relieved the heaviness of my heart. Dispensing praise was naturally not easy, and so I adopted the mask of my doctor's authority, to hide my embarrassment, and said rather gruffly,

"That may be so, but now I have to get you to bed. If we walk to Tooley Street or Queen Elizabeth Street, we will surely find a hansom, to bring us to Baker Street. If I support you, can you walk that far?"

"I am sure I can," he said rather thinly, and smiled as we set off.

Conclusion

Despite all my skills as a doctor, arguing that Holmes should stay in bed, he would not. I was therefore relieved that he at least agreed to rest on the sofa and read "The Times." Even so, he could not conceal that he fell asleep at intervals and did not concentrate on his reading. I sat alongside him and read in the poetry book I had already started the evening before. I could thus at regular intervals look towards him and assess critically his progress. He agreed that at one moment the calm of the salon could be disturbed, as Mrs. Hudson brought a light meal for us. It was good to see that the feeling of sickness of which he at first complained, clearly resulting from the shock, was now past, and he was at least able to enjoy Mrs. Hudson's cucumber sandwiches.

It was already late in the afternoon when I heard the doorbell, and then heavy steps climbed the stair to our floor. At the knock on our door, I called the visitor to enter, and first came Mrs. Hudson, closely followed by Inspectors Lestrade and Gregson.

"Dr. Watson, please forgive me, I told the two gentlemen that Mr. Holmes is unwell, but they are most anxious to speak with him."

But the good lady came no further, for Holmes leapt up, as if on a spring, and announced with his full energy, "Mrs. Hudson, I am completely recovered, and I may not allow the two inspectors from Scotland Yard to be kept waiting."

Mrs. Hudson sighed deeply and stepped back to allow the two policemen to enter. There was a brief silence, and then Holmes addressed them directly.

"Thank you both, gentlemen, for keeping your word, so that I can now perhaps question the man who was arrested. Should I come with you now?"

As my friend said this, his eyes showed his eager anticipation. The expressions of our two visitors changed, however, in a moment, from indifference to embarrassed.

"I fear we have come, Mr. Holmes, to tell you that a conversation with the man arrested yesterday at Tower Bridge will not be possible."

Inspector Lestrade struggled for words and looked at Gregson for help.

Gregson cleared his throat, and then added to Lestrade's comment, "There has been a most regrettable accident, Mr. Holmes. The arrested man was lodged in one of our cells, and succeeded in lighting a fire. He perhaps hoped thereby that when it was noticed, and the cell door opened, he would in the general confusion have a chance to escape. It is a trick that many have tried, and one or two may have succeeded. But this time it failed. The fire was noticed, the alarm was given, and it was quickly extinguished, but by this time the arrested man was already too severely burned to survive. Such a thing really must not be allowed to happen. It is undoubtedly a case of negligence, and we will have to take disciplinary measures with the warder."

While Gregson said this, I saw how Holmes' enthusiasm broke down. It was as if a burning candle had been extinguished. Lestrade and Gregson realised too, what an effect their words had had. Nervously, they went on talking,

"It is reassuring that we will not be held responsible, for he was Superintendent Melville's prisoner. We had proposed to take him to Scotland Yard, first, for interrogation." Lestrade's explanation did little to clear the air.

Gregson continued, "We are really most sorry, Mr. Holmes, that we cannot therefore help you further. You had after all been so helpful in clearing up the death of Joseph Healy. And you have certainly contributed to ensuring that the attack on the Prince of Wales and his guests could not succeed."

Holmes showed not the slightest interest in these comments but went on looking absently out of the window. The two Inspectors fingered their hats, and I decided that I would thank them for their call and show them out. The visit was at an end. Visibly relieved, they took their leave hastily.

Now that we were alone, Holmes took down his violin, sat down cross-legged on the sofa, and began to generate fearful and melancholy sounds. I sat for a while passing in review all that we had seen and heard in thcse last forty-eight hours. I had hardly slept, I was at the scene of a gruesome murder, and had with Holmes been in places I would never have sought out for myself. I had been at times at the limit of my physical and also nervous strength. You might imagine that it was now my wish, to return to Kensington and to resume my quiet and ordered life as a doctor.

It was, however, not so. I found, dear reader, that my first wish was quite the opposite. I had to admit that I had enjoyed the experience of these two days. There was however something more to hold me. It was the moment in the sordid street near the Thames, the moment when I had attempted, with my army revolver, to protect my friend. I knew then that his judgment was correct. I was his friend and comrade, and I could not flinch from his side.

The succession of painful sounds, which he was still extracting from his violin, became suddenly even less harmonious, and I knew that depression was overcoming him. It was time to break the mood, and to tell him what I had decided, in the hope that he would approve.

"Holmes," I said firmly, "my mind is made up. I am going to sell up my practice and my home in Kensington and come back to live here in Baker Street with you."

As I said this, the scraping of the violin stopped abruptly. Holmes lifted his head, and I saw his eyes shining brightly. A satisfied smile broke out over that tormented face.

"Wonderful, Watson," he called out with delight and added, "That is really very good news, for which I could never have hoped. I would suggest that we go out to celebrate at once, with dinner at Simpson's."

"I can think of nothing better," I replied, and wondered at the way in which joy and pleasure suddenly changed Holmes' complete being.

Dinner at Simpson's was as always excellent, and our discussion, which dwelt neither upon the failed dynamite plot, nor upon the murder of Joseph Healy, was at the same level of excellence. I had thought, given that Holmes was still to a degree convalescent, that we should not tax his strength more than necessary, and so we did not linger at Simpson's but made our way back to Baker Street, to enjoy a quiet whisky in our lounge. Holmes welcomed the proposal, and so we were soon again in our armchairs by the fireplace.

Before we could raise our glasses, however, there was a knock on the door, and Mrs. Hudson appeared at the door, with the news that a gentleman wished urgently to speak to us. I saw Holmes' eyes light up with interest, and I knew then that I did not have to fear for his strength. He turned to me to say, "Perhaps it is a new client. When someone calls at this hour, it must be important."

"Then you should receive him, Holmes," I replied.

A few moments later, a rather heavily built man of a certain age entered our room, and introduced himself as Henry Beckett, a manager of the jewellery and watchmaking business of Frodsham and Co., in the Strand. Holmes invited him to take a seat and then asked, "And how can I be of service to you, Mr. Beckett?"

Mr. Beckett looked thoughtfully at Holmes and said, "I think it is rather I, who can be of service to you." Somewhat surprised, we looked at our visitor, who now offered us an explanation.

"I should perhaps first recall to you that Frodsham & Co. is not only concerned with the sale and purchase of watches, but also with their care and repair. This work often brings musical boxes into our hands. These have mechanisms which have much in common with those of watches and clocks. In many cases, of course, a musical box is much more complicated than a watch. It is an aspect of our work which I find particularly attractive. It is therefore one of my responsibilities, to attend to our business with the cleaning and repair of such musical boxes. Today I had a customer, a gentleman whom I did not know, who, came in shortly before I was intending to close the shop, He asked me to repair a musical box. As I took it in my hands, my heart beat faster, for it was clearly an example of a very fine piece of Geneva or London workmanship.

"I opened it in the gentleman's presence, I saw that the defect was not serious, and that it could readily be corrected. I told him so, and said that I would deal with it, inviting him to come by on Monday morning to collect it and pay for the repair. He explained however that was not to his liking, since he was about to leave London. He asked me to estimate quickly the cost, which I did and he paid without question. As I took his payment, I saw at once that the amount rewarded us most generously, but he admitted no discussion. He then explained that it was intended for you, and, when I had made the repair, I was to bring it directly here to you."

As he finished this explanation, he took from his pocket a small box, and opened it to show an oval ornamental musical box, which was decorated beautifully with enamel paintings. He offered it to Holmes, saying, "The gentleman also left a letter for you, which I was to give you with the musical box. He left me with a clear instruction that you were first to read the letter, and then to open the musical box."

Mr. Beckett reached into an inner pocket, to extract a closed envelope, addressed to Holmes. This he also carefully placed in Holmes' hands.

"Mr. Beckett, could you perhaps describe your client, who gave you this task?"

"I am a specialist for watches and mechanisms, but less so, I fear, for persons. Let me try. He is about as big as you, Mr. Holmes, and strongly built. I did not see much of his face, for he had a dark full beard and dark bushy eyebrows. He also wore dark sunglasses, which surprised me as we are of course in London, and not in the Alps where it might be more usual. His dress was very correct and of the highest quality. I also had the thought that he was perhaps German."

"Indeed?" asked Holmes with interest.

"I could not pretend to be quite certain, but it seemed to me that his English, which was beyond reproach, was just slightly coloured with a German accent. You will understand that in our business we have regular contacts with, for example, the German watchmakers Junghans, and I therefore often hear German accents."

Holmes nodded approvingly to Mr. Beckett's words, and then asked, "Is there anything about this person that you might add?"

"No, Mr. Holmes, I think that is all. And if you will now excuse me, I ought to get home, to my wife and children."

"Of course, Mr. Beckett," replied Holmes, "and I am most grateful to you." and he asked me to show our visitor out. I thus left the lounge with him, also thanking him profusely.

When I returned, I found that Holmes had already opened the envelope and was looking thoughtfully at the letter now in his hands. "Do you now know who has given you this rare and beautiful object?" I asked. He did not answer, but put the letter in my hands, while reaching for his magnifying glass to study the musical box. I took the letter and read:

Mr. Holmes,
Once more our paths have crossed, although you will not know how we learned of your involvement. This time you have the honour of victory. I have to tell you that I am slowly beginning to understand our mutual acquaintance, the late Professor. He had much earlier recognised that there is rarely

an opportunity to pit one's own intellect against a partner on the same level. I am certain that you know who has addressed this note to you. Should you doubt, the musical box, which I give you, will make everything clear.

This was troubling, but I still had no suspicion. Holmes however lifted the lid, which allowed a gentle and melodious tune to be played. Holmes looked into the instrument, and I saw how his eyes and lips tightened. Then he opened his eyes fully, smiled and looked at me. I asked whether I might see for myself. Without a further word he offered me the musical box. I almost dropped it in surprise. The interior displayed a rustic landscape, in enamel painting, before which there were two figures, driven by a clockwork mechanism. One was kneeling, the other turning a large wheel. By means of a delicate chain, the large wheel drove a small grindstone, on which the kneeling figure was sharpening a blade.

"It is the German Knife-Grinder again!" I gasped. I could scarcely believe it.

Holmes was already lost in thought. My ideas were racing. The German Knife-Grinder, a sinister person whom we had never seen, was here in London, involved in a plot to murder the Prince of Wales and those near to him. What could that mean? And was he perhaps the one who had ordered the murder of Reuben Healy when he became a nuisance? And then the prisoner in the burning cell: Had this man had him killed to silence him? But all this meant that the mysterious Knife-Grinder, whoever he was, already had a powerful criminal network in London and elsewhere. Who was he, and what was he doing here?

I thought back to Holmes' explanations of two nights ago, and of the missing papers, which Moriarty was so desperate to find in Meiringen three years ago before he died. If these had come into the Knife-Grinder's hands, then, knowing the Professor was dead, he had every means to build up again the criminal network which once was Moriarty's. Perhaps all was not lost in the great Meiringen fire? Perhaps the Knife-Grinder had gone back to look, before the fire. Perhaps he had the fire started at his own orders, to give the impression that all was destroyed. My fantasy was running wild, when I heard Holmes' sober voice.

"It seems we might have interesting times before us, Watson, and there are people whom we do not know, playing for very high stakes. If this plot had succeeded, half the states of Europe would have been up in arms. I do not like it at all. We came into the story only because Gregson called us to Joseph Healy's murder, rightly fearing that it was not a trivial affair, and two days later all is over. We may never know why the attack was here attempted, nor who might have been behind it. Who had commissioned the Knife-Grinder to make such an attempt? Superintendent Melville certainly knows more. Again, we have said nothing, but already they, whoever they are, know we were involved. This is a sinister prospect. Is it still, despite this, your intention to move in here and keep me company?"

"My mind is indeed made up," I replied firmly.

"Then, my friend, let us raise our glasses and drink a toast to our friendship and to your new start here," said Holmes.

I raised my glass willingly, and added, "And to all that might await us!"

End

Also from Johanna M. Rieke

Do you love Cornwall, with its cliffs and breakers, sleepy fishing harbours and villages? Would you like to meet a real English Lord? And do you enjoy an authentic, well researched historical crime story? With the author you will accompany the renowned Baker Street detective, Sherlock Holmes, and his friend Dr Watson, on their journey to Cornwall. There, in idyllic surroundings, they are faced with seemingly impenetrable questions, leading to desperate villainy. A fifty-year-old history of intrigue, smuggling, betrayal, murder and revenge waits to be revealed, and you are there, with Holmes and Watson.

Also from Johanna M. Rieke

London in 1890 is shocked by a series of gruesome murders. There seems to be no rhyme or reason to them, except for their location in the Thames dockland. Scotland Yard is perplexed. Can Sherlock Holmes and Dr Watson help before worse follows? And what is really going on? Author Johanna Rieke brings rich and poor in Victorian London realistically to life, as she unfolds for you the surprising story of the Thames Murders, as disaster is averted at the last moment.

Also from Johanna M. Rieke

It is summer in 1890, in Robertsbridge, a small village in East Sussex. Dr Watson, on holiday without Holmes, finds the village peaceful and sleepy, but the truth is different. He soon discovers that the villagers are afraid, the atmosphere is threatening. Why do three mysterious white monks haunt the ruined abbey? What does the gipsy seek? Where is a missing ten-year-old boy? Watson calls for Holmes, but why is Holmes fearful of endangering lives? We read in this exciting story how Holmes' patient deduction and Watson's courage come together, to solve a many-sided mystery just before it turns into disaster.

Also from Johanna M. Rieke

We are in London in 1890, and the British Museum plans to exhibit the contents, brought specially to London, of a newly excavated Egyptian tomb. The event is disturbed by the murder of a museum watchman. A suspect is quickly found, a young museum assistant, caught red-handed with a bloodstained knife. But things are not so simple; behind this apparently clear case Holmes uncovers, piece by piece, just as did the archaeologists, a complicated story of blackmail, violence and treachery, which, at every step, threatens him, and Watson, with deadly consequences. See how events ranging from the British Embassy in Cairo to a theatre in East London can baffle and confuse, until Holmes and Watson find the last pieces of the puzzle, and must fight for their lives.

MX Publishing

MX Publishing brings the best in new Sherlock Holmes novels, biographies, graphic novels and short story collections every month. With over 400 books it's the largest catalogue of new Sherlock Holmes books in the world.

We have over one hundred and fifty Holmes authors. The majority of our authors write new Holmes fiction - in all genres from very traditional pastiches through to modern novels, fantasy, crossover, children's books and humour.

In Holmes biography we have award winning historians including Alistair Duncan, Paul R Spiring, and Brian W Pugh

MX Publishing also has one of the largest communities of Holmes fans on Facebook and Twitter under @mxpublishing.

www.ingramcontent.com/pod-product-compliance
Lightning Source LLC
Chambersburg PA
CBHW070616310726
48982CB00001B/102

* 9 7 8 1 8 0 4 2 4 0 9 6 0 *